THE
JOURNEY
PRIZE

STORIES

WINNERS OF THE $10,000 JOURNEY PRIZE

1989: Holley Rubinsky for "Rapid Transits"

1990: Cynthia Flood for "My Father Took a Cake to France"

1991: Yann Martel for "The Facts Behind the Helsinki Roccamatios"

1992: Rozena Maart for "No Rosa, No District Six"

1993: Gayla Reid for "Sister Doyle's Men"

1994: Melissa Hardy for "Long Man the River"

1995: Kathryn Woodward for "Of Marranos and Gilded Angels"

1996: Elyse Gasco for "Can You Wave Bye Bye, Baby?"

1997 (shared): Gabriella Goliger for "Maladies of the Inner Ear"
Anne Simpson for "Dreaming Snow"

1998: John Brooke for "The Finer Points of Apples"

1999: Alissa York for "The Back of the Bear's Mouth"

2000: Timothy Taylor for "Doves of Townsend"

2001: Kevin Armstrong for "The Cane Field"

2002: Jocelyn Brown for "Miss Canada"

2003: Jessica Grant for "My Husband's Jump"

2004: Devin Krukoff for "The Last Spark"

2005: Matt Shaw for "Matchbook for a Mother's Hair"

2006: Heather Birrell for "BriannaSusannaAlana"

2007: Craig Boyko for "OZY"

2008: Saleema Nawaz for "My Three Girls"

2009: Yasuko Thanh for "Floating Like the Dead"

2010: Devon Code for "Uncle Oscar"

2011: Miranda Hill for "Petitions to Saint Chronic"

2012: Alex Pugsley for "Crisis on Earth-X"

2013: Naben Ruthnum for "Cinema Rex"

2014: Tyler Keevil for "Sealskin"

2015: Deirdre Dore for "The Wise Baby"

2016: Colette Langlois for "The Emigrants"

The BEST of CANADA'S NEW WRITERS

THE
JOURNEY
PRIZE

STORIES

SELECTED BY
KEVIN HARDCASTLE
GRACE O'CONNELL
AYELET TSABARI

McCLELLAND & STEWART

Library and Archives Canada Cataloguing in Publication is available upon request

Published simultaneously in the United States of America by McClelland & Stewart, a Penguin Random House Company

Library of Congress Control Number is available upon request

ISBN: 978-0-7710-4820-3
ebook ISBN: 978-0-7710-4821-0

The quotations from *Of the Nature of Things* by Lucretius that appear in "The Nature of Things" are taken from the translations by Ronald Melville (Oxford University Press, 2009) and by William Ellery Leonard.

Typeset in Janson by M&S, Toronto
Printed and bound in the United States of America

McClelland & Stewart,
a division of Penguin Random House Canada Limited,
a Penguin Random House Company
www.penguinrandomhouse.ca

1 2 3 4 5   21 20 19 18 17

Penguin
Random House
McCLELLAND & STEWART

ABOUT THE JOURNEY PRIZE STORIES

The $10,000 Journey Prize is awarded annually to an emerging writer of distinction. This award, now in its twenty-ninth year, and given for the seventeenth time in association with the Writers' Trust of Canada as the Writers' Trust of Canada/ McClelland & Stewart Journey Prize, is made possible by James A. Michener's generous donation of his Canadian royalty earnings from his novel *Journey*, published by McClelland & Stewart in 1988. The Journey Prize itself is the most significant monetary award given in Canada to a developing writer for a short story or excerpt from a fiction work in progress. The winner of this year's Journey Prize will be selected from among the ten stories in this book.

The Journey Prize Stories has established itself as the most prestigious annual fiction anthology in the country, introducing readers to the finest new literary writers from coast to coast for more than two decades. It has become a who's who of up-and-coming writers, and many of the authors who have appeared in the anthology's pages have gone on to distinguish themselves with short story collections, novels, and literary awards. The anthology comprises a selection from submissions made by the editors of literary journals from across the country, who have chosen what, in their view, is the most exciting writing in English that they have published in the previous year. In recognition of the vital role journals play in fostering literary voices, McClelland & Stewart makes its own award of $2,000 to the journal that originally published and submitted the winning entry.

This year the selection jury comprised three acclaimed writers:

Kevin Hardcastle is a fiction writer from Simcoe County, Ontario. He is the author of the novel *In the Cage* and the short story collection *Debris*, which won the Trillium Book Award and the ReLit Award for Short Fiction, was a runner-up for the Danuta Gleed Literary Award, and a finalist for the Kobo Emerging Writer Prize. Hardcastle's short fiction has been widely published in Canada and the United States, in journals such as *The Malahat Review*, *The New Quarterly*, *The Puritan*, *EVENT*, and *Shenandoah*. His writing has been anthologized in *The Journey Prize Stories 24* and *26*, *Best Canadian Stories 15*, and *Internazionale*. He lives and works in Toronto.

Grace O'Connell is the author of the novels *Be Ready for the Lightning* and *Magnified World*, the latter of which was a national bestseller and a *Globe and Mail 100* selected book. She was the 2014 winner of the Canadian Authors Association Emerging Writer Award, and her work has appeared in publications such as the *Globe and Mail*, the *National Post*, *ELLE Canada*, *This Magazine*, *The Journey Prize Stories 24*, and *Taddle Creek*, where she previously served as Associate Editor. She holds an MFA in creative writing and teaches at the University of Toronto while working as a freelance writer and editor.

Ayelet Tsabari was born in Israel to a large family of Yemeni descent. Her first book, *The Best Place on Earth*, won the Sami Rohr Prize for Jewish Literature and the Edward Lewis Wallant Award, and was long listed for the Frank O'Connor International Short Story Award. The book was a *New York Times Book Review* Editors' Choice, a *Kirkus Reviews* Best Book of 2016, and has been published internationally to great acclaim. Excerpts from her forthcoming book have won a National Magazine Award and a Western Magazine Award. She lives in Toronto.

The jury read a total of eighty-five submissions without knowing the names of the authors or those of the journals in which the stories originally appeared. McClelland & Stewart would like to thank the jury for their efforts in selecting this year's anthology and, ultimately, the winner of this year's Journey Prize.

McClelland & Stewart would also like to acknowledge the continuing enthusiastic support of writers, literary journal editors, and the public in the common celebration of new voices in Canadian fiction.

For more information about *The Journey Prize Stories*, please visit www.facebook.com/TheJourneyPrize.

CONTENTS

INTRODUCTION

Short fiction is an unforgiving form. And that's what makes it so fantastic. A great short story has memorable, unique characters, a plot that readers can't look away from, and gorgeous, essential language—all contained in a stack of pages that's usually thinner than a toonie. Getting to the core of an emotional landscape in just a few thousand words is a feat to be savoured and celebrated.

Short fiction is the gymnastics of writing: technical, demanding, and, when done well, looks effortless. But writers know that writing an excellent story is the furthest thing from effortless. The short story is prose at its most distilled, and luckily for readers, Canada is as good at distilling fiction as we are at distilling even boozier materials.

As writers, readers, and lovers of the short story, we were thrilled to be asked to put together the anthology you hold in your hands, which meant reading some of the finest short fiction published in Canadian literary magazines in the previous year. We each came into this process with our own notions of what makes a good story: a strong, clear voice, finely honed technique, and well-crafted characters. In the end, the ten stories we selected were the ones that gripped, moved, surprised, and inspired us—and stayed with us long after reading. The stories varied in style and tone, subject matter and sensibility. If we had to choose one distinct quality that defined these stories as a group and set them apart from the other submissions, it would be an undefined "aliveness"—that singular, elusive characteristic that told us we were in the presence of something special. We are proud that these stories prove that there continues to be an infusion of new talent into our literary community.

Sharon Bala's "Butter Tea at Starbucks" ambitiously and seamlessly weaves together the personal and the political, the mundane and the momentous, and does so in beautifully crafted prose. Bala has an ear for dialogue, a keen eye for detail, and a perceptive, merciless gaze that makes for complex and deeply flawed characters. The result is remarkable, at once delightful and unsettling. Notably, Bala is the only author with multiple stories included in this collection. Her second Journey Prize selection, "Reading Week," is a story built on subtlety and understated emotion, yet one that still manages to move the reader and foster a real sense of loss and longing. The writing elevates what, on the surface, appears to be a seemingly ordinary story into a narrative that is rich and quietly profound.

Michael Meagher's "Used to It" delves expertly into the lives of the working class, and explores the peculiarities and harsh demands of the hard, physical labour that the protagonist does to keep a roof over his head. The writing is rugged and muscular, but still lends dignity to the story's rough cast of characters. The dialogue and description kept us enthralled throughout, and the world that the author depicts is painfully real.

There isn't a word wasted in **Sarah Kabamba**'s nuanced "They Come Crying." Kabamba writes with an assured hand, using restrained, evocative prose to portray the rituals of grief as seen through a child's eyes, while illuminating the cultural gaps common within immigrant families, and the power of food and stories to bridge them.

Jack Wang's "The Nature of Things" pushes the limits of the short story by spanning generations and continents. The tale of two Chinese-Canadian lovers who travel to Shanghai and find themselves caught in the Second Sino-Japanese War is so epic in scope that it reads almost like a mini-novel. Wang employs rich imagery, lyrical language, and a wistful tone to evoke a tumultuous time and place in history.

The unnamed child narrator in **Patrick Doerksen**'s "Leech" is unforgettable. The monster of the story is truly chilling, and the central metaphor is handled deftly and nimbly. Balancing innovation with emotion, it's a deceptively simple story that hits the bull's eye perfectly.

"A Girl and a Dog on a Friday Night" is another story that looks beyond the mundane particulars of everyday life to uncover the potential for catastrophe and ruin that exists in the lives of those who have slipped between the cracks. The opening scene is tense, and the narrative is increasingly unpredictable and surprising. **Kelly Ward** captures the truth of a young mother's struggle without being heavy-handed or forcing our focus. Instead, the reader is drawn naturally, and with great concern, into the life of the protagonist and her daughter.

In "Subject Winifred," **Maria Reva** creates an unusual framing device to tell the story of a precocious child who is as endearing as she is tragic, and whose obsession with keeping tally of everything—from how many times she's woken up since birth to the number of days her mother has been in a relationship with God—helps her make sense of a chaotic home life. The story stood out for its immediacy, for its distinct voice, and for Reva's skill in building tension throughout the fragmented narrative, leading to an inevitable, though no less shocking, conclusion.

A beautiful, sometimes masterfully raw journey, "She Is Water" is a story that we felt in our bones even before **Darlene Naponse** told it. The unsentimental depiction of life in a remote First Nations community distinguishes this story, as does the way small joys and major tragedies are handled with equal measures of empathy and clear-sightedness; they flow over the reader as water might.

There's so much quiet confidence on display in "Old Growth" by **Lisa Alward**. This is a writer who knows what she is doing; there's an old-school attention to craft and line-by-line quality, but the story feels absolutely fresh and contemporary. As a reader, you simply feel you are in good hands with Alward.

We invite you to read these stories and add these names to your list of authors to keep an eye on. The skill, vision, and dedication required to write the best short stories provides a writer with a set of tools that they will carry with them throughout their careers. And we truly believe the writers in this anthology are positioned to use those tools and their talent to add something special to our national literature. We would encourage the writers who narrowly missed the cut to keep working on and sharing their stories. The well is deep, and we are certain that those who did not make it into these pages will fill them up in the years to come.

We want to honour the writers whose stories made such an impact on us this year, and we are proud to present them here. This anthology is a celebration of the strength and dexterity of our short story writers, and shows the promising future of Canadian literature.

Kevin Hardcastle
Grace O'Connell
Ayelet Tsabari
June 2017

SHARON BALA

BUTTER TEA AT STARBUCKS

The flames flap with a noise like laundry on a line. The fire is an orange column. A plastic bag pirouettes in mid-air. The camera, unsteady, lingers and lingers. And in the middle, the figure stands upright, stoic or suicidal. Pema thinks: She's already dead.

There's a blizzard. Jamal's voice, through the phone, is in her left ear.

Pema looks away from the TV. In the waiting room people slump into the plastic chairs, turning the pages of the *Toronto Sun* or *Today's Parent*. Outside the black window, snow whirls like a thousand dervishes.

Here too, she says. Pearson is closed.

I can't believe I'm going to miss it, Jamal says.

Pema wants to ask Jamal, Have you seen the news? But of course he hasn't. He's got other things to think about and now so does she. The intercom pages Dr. Patel to Maternity.

They're calling the doctor, Pema says. I have to go. I'll text you. Think of a name.

———

Karma's room smells like blood and shit. There is a beeping machine and an impassive nurse in a hairnet and blue booties. Pema has never heard her sister make noises like this before. Urgent, animal sounds that roar out from some place deep inside that Pema had not known existed. She wants to call their mother, but Karma says no in her big sister don't-fuck-with-me-now voice.

Jamal sends impotent texts. Pema's pocket buzzes. A little envelope lands on the screen.

He says he loves you. She holds up the phone so Karma can see that he has spelled out all the words.

I love you. I love you. What else is there to say? The wind howls and the ambulances scream as Karma bears down. And Pema is repulsed and terrified. Because the room is hot, damp. It is a jungle, raw and wild. And how could this be? No, it could not be Karma, who, age sixteen, looked Amala and Pala straight in the eyes and said, I will do exactly as I like. Just you try to stop me. Battle cries, a warrior in the throes of death. The phone in Pema's pocket, demanding attention. The nurse and now the doctor saying, One more push. And Karma sitting up, her body yawning open, reaching down, the crown of flattened jet-black hair. And the nurse asking, Can you see it? forcing Pema to look, even though she doesn't want to, swallowing back bile. And the storm and the people in the hallway and the green line spiking up, diving down, running straight. And finally, finally, the small mewling cry. And Pema overcome with sobs that heave out of her mouth, joy bursting from every orifice, taking her by surprise.

———

Karma sleeps, deflated, defeated, and Pema takes photos of the baby, trying to forget what she has witnessed. Karma's mouth contorting, her feet in the air, knees spread wide.

The baby has a cone for a head. She looks red and weary, battered from the ordeal of coming into existence. The nurse hands over the bundle and Pema is amazed by her lightness, the seven pounds and three ounces barely registering in her arms. She holds her niece awkwardly, terrified of snapping her neck.

What's her name?

They haven't decided. Pema doesn't tell the nurse that the Dalai Lama has been asked to weigh in on the decision.

Instead, she hides in the bathroom and calls her mother.

Does the baby look like him? Amala asks.

She's healthy, Pema says. And so cute. They speak in Tibetan. We've received word from Kundun.

Ma, Pema says in English. Karma and Jamal are choosing a name.

She emerges from the bathroom to find her sister is awake, sitting up in bed with the baby.

Let me guess, Karma says. Tenzin? Figures.

Pema hadn't told her about the call. She had tried her best to whisper into the phone. Karma knew all.

Karma holds the baby like a football. She opens the hospital gown and one breast flops out. The breast is engorged and veiny, the aureole like a dinner plate. Pema wants to avert her eyes. She suggests Maya. After Lord Buddha's mother. Or Trinley? We could call her Trin.

But Karma says no. No Tibetan names. She frowns and jostles, struggling to line up an elongated nipple with the baby's rosebud lips.

Pema has never met a Tibetan who didn't have a Tib name. She says to her sister: Don't shut them out.

The baby opens her mouth; milk dribbles down her chin. Karma mutters: Latch! Latch! The baby turns her head away. Karma says, They started it.

Karma works with rare books at the university library. Jamal makes documentaries. Their professions are nouns: librarian, filmmaker. Pema types numbers into columns. She has only a verb: data entry.

At lunchtime, the lowest rungs go down the street to the cafeteria in the *Toronto Sun* building, where they bitch about their bosses and commiserate about being the working poor. The others are Amanda, Brenda, and Ling-Mei. Pema never feels comfortable around Ling-Mei, even though their desks are beside each other.

Brenda says the guy at the falafel shop is Tibetan. Ling-Mei says, No! He's like sixteen. Pema plays along, rolling her eyes and laughing. She wants to fast-forward ten years, get to the part where she has a family and a house, a noun on a business card.

When Pema thinks about her life—straight As, failing beginner piano, eating sandwiches under the stairwell—all of it leading to this moment at four fifty-five when her boss tells her that there is an urgent deliverable, she feels like she's been tricked. But when Karma looks up, harried, from the squalling infant and asks, How was work? Pema always says: Fine. Same old.

Amala wants to know if she has made any new friends. What she means is, Has Pema met any boys?

I'm busy with the baby, Pema says. She has lived in Toronto for a year but she has not yet been to the Tibetan Community Centre. Whenever she thinks of it, she imagines moon-faced FOBs. Wandering souls.

Just date whoever you like, Karma says. If they wanted us to marry Tibs, they shouldn't have left Dharamsala.

The Chinese are taking over Tibet, moving in on state-sponsored programs to dilute the population. They run the businesses; they drive up inflation. And more and more Tibs dispersing into exile.

We are like the Jews. Pala, unchecked, is something else altogether. He could have been a Baptist preacher. Look at what they did to my parents, he says. The Chinese would exterminate us all if they could.

They had kidnapped the Panchen Lama. What kind of government steals a religion's chosen one? China said *they* would be the ones to choose the Kundun's replacement. Whenever Pala got on this tangent, spit started flying. The arrogance! What if Berlusconi announced he was going to choose the next pope? Impossible!

It is Pema's duty to marry a Tibetan, to have sweet-faced almond-skinned children. She wants to do her part. But when she plays scrabble with Jamal and Karma, she wants what they have too.

Find a Tibetan? Karma raises one eyebrow high on her forehead; the eyebrow says *I'm above all this nonsense*. Here? That's like going into Starbucks and ordering butter tea.

Ugh.

Now, now, Karma says. That's your heritage!

———

It takes the burning woman three days to die. Pema thinks of her children, now motherless, and her skin, charred like a drumstick forgotten on a barbecue. And what it all means, to become a human torch, a beacon for a cause.

It is March and the city has had enough of winter. Pema scratches at the frost on the window, feeling the ice collect under her thumbnail. Behind her, Karma rocks the baby. But her soothing murmurs are drowned out by the tortured wail.

The dog is called Fatty Bolger. He sits in the narrow hallway, warming his nose between his paws, and looks up at Pema with big, mournful eyes. The baby's cry could break your heart. Her head is flung back in abandon, her tiny lungs unequal to her despair. It's not colic or hunger. It's not a foul diaper.

Karma looks to Pema and begs, What should I do?

Pema does not recognize this tearful, needy sister.

Put her in the stroller, Pema suggests. She takes the dog's leash off the hook by the door. Let's try a walk.

But when it comes to the baby, Karma is afraid. No, she says. It's too slippery. The ice. It's not safe.

Pema takes the dog instead. He droops and sways low to the ground, his nose leading the way. There's a whole world of smells, Karma had said once. We have no idea.

Pema keeps one hand on his leash and waves with the other to the neighbours as she negotiates bumpy patches of ice. In Medicine Hat, where she grew up, they were the only Tibetan family. She still catches herself staring when she sees other Tibs. Their corner of the city is peppered with exiles. On Wednesdays the Tibetan shops and take-outs are always full.

Fatty Bolger is not a Lhasa Apso. He is not called Choden or Tsering like the other dogs on their street. But everyone knows they are Tibetan by the multicoloured squares of the prayer flag that garland the front door.

The house is like a supermodel—tall and skinny with brittle bones. On the top floor, in what used to be the attic, the slanted roof leaks. A white plastic rain gutter runs like a tunnel, flush with the ceiling. There is a bucket in the corner and a string that hangs down to it, anchored by a rock. An indoor waterfall every time it rains.

Pema's room is on this floor, across from an alcove where she and Karma kneel once a day. Lord Buddha sits cross-legged on a low wooden table. A flower floats in a shallow dish. Pema fills six bowls with water every morning and Karma empties them at night. Pema has forgotten the meaning of this ritual but she likes it anyway, just as she likes the silk embroidered thangka that hangs over the table. A monster devours the wheel of life. Concentric rings, each one circling the other like a trap, and the three poisons in the centre. Ignorance, hatred, and greed chasing their own tails.

There have been calls to boycott the Olympics. Controversy swirling and the Games only a few months away. In the end, Pema knows that none of it will matter. Skeletons turning to dust in the closet while the world oohs and aahs at the opening ceremonies. The dancing, the ribbons, the smoke and the mirrors. What Beijing excels at: putting on a show.

China has declared self-immolation a crime. The monks are banned from offering condolences or conducting prayers for the dead. When Karma chants, her voice rumbles deep and trance-like. Pema, in bed, cuddles up with a hot water bottle. She keeps the door open and listens to her sister. Once a day, Karma is herself again, reliable and constant.

Om mani peme hung. Karma intones with a slow and steady beat. *Om mani peme hung.* The syllables of the mantra fill up the room, seem to fill up the whole world. Coaxing one to sleep, another toward enlightenment. Urging them both, Step away from the light.

What had the woman thought of as she stood choking in the flames? A dream of homeland or her children. Or maybe the overwhelming agony had been everything. The sear and singe and the smoke. Maybe she was wishing she had not woken up that morning.

The pipes have burst. Jamal and Pema wear Wellingtons. Water steams around their ankles. Pema tries not to think about rats, long tails swishing around corners in the subterranean dark. Her steps are hesitant. She imagines waterlogged fur, a hump of resistance, thin bones snapping under her rubber sole.

The copper pipes sputter and piss in streams. Towels wrapped around them bulge and drip. Pema wrings out her mop. The water in the bucket is slicked with grease. Jamal holds the baby monitor sideways across his mouth. Call the plumber, he says into the static.

Jamal is home for another weekend. Brunch was his idea, the baby's first outing. Karma was resistant. Take her, she said. Go without me. Even though they all knew this was impossible. Karma is still trying to breast-feed and the baby is permanently attached to her, a tiny, grasping marsupial. When the wet spots appeared on the front of Karma's shirt, she had cried and said, I knew it. We shouldn't have come.

Pema had never seen Karma cry before. She had raised a hand for the bill and locked the car seat into the stroller because those were the things she knew how to do. The heat wasn't working when they got home and that's when they realized about the pipes.

Through the monitor, they can hear the baby fussing. Karma doesn't take her voice up an octave or call the baby *baba* or *monchie* when she consoles her. Pema thinks that if she did these things the baby would not cry so often. She thinks it but she does not say it.

Pema is relieved that Jamal is here, to take charge of her leaky sister and the weeping pipes. Jamal's hair is clipped short. His teeth flash white against his dark skin.

We need more towels, he says to Pema.

There is a teddy-bear-shaped scar on Jamal's back. When Amala first met him, she had said, astonished: But, Karma, he looks like a monkey.

Sometimes Pema takes the night shift and sleeps with the monitor. Fatty Bolger sits by her feet at the fire. Or paces with her as she coos and pats the baby's rustling bum. Jamal made a cradle. Pema rocks it with her foot as she streams the news from Tibet.

Lhasa is a grey-brown blur, the shell of a city. Objects are flung at the Bank of China building. A woman points to an overturned truck: *The Tibetans are not blameless; they have blood on their hands.* A baby carriage tips dangerously off a curb. A man brings his fist down over and over. The camera watches from a rooftop, lens aimed like a sniper.

The images are grainy. They require translation. The Al Jazeera reporter speaks in un-accented English: Beijing is blaming the Dalai Lama. She demonstrates how censors black out the international channels. China is a brat with his fingers in his ears. Pema wants to smack him.

An American pundit with an earpiece: If we in the free world don't speak out, we have lost all moral authority. And Kundun with his massive glasses, old grandfather's face like a creased pillow, leaning down, whispering into the bandages. *Do not pass over with hatred in your heart.*

The young mother burns again and again. Every time Pema watches the footage, she hits replay on her suffering.

When Jamal calls from Halifax, they put him on speaker. There is a snow plow in the background. He opens a beer and they hear that too—the fizz of the steam when he twists off the cap.

Tell me, he says, and Pema gives him a rundown of the vitals. Up every three hours. Another pound gained. No sign of colic.

She hates my breasts, Karma wails into the phone.

Formula, Jamal says. It didn't hurt me.

Pema touches the baby's cheek with the back of her finger. The baby is sleeping but she can't help herself. Her skin is impossibly soft. She holds the phone so Jamal can hear her breathing. Jamal says: Alpha Bravo Charlie. Sleep through the night. That's an order. Do you copy?

Pema does not tell him that she had found Karma standing, stiff over the crib, while the baby bawled in a rage. Toothless red gums, each cry forced out with a great panting effort. She does not tell him how Karma had turned to her and said: Sometimes I fantasize about being in an accident. Just so someone else would take care of her.

Pema had replaced the sodden diaper, her fingers fumbling with the tape, while the baby fell asleep, exhausted, on the change table. Pema knows her sister didn't mean it. No one can be held accountable for the words that break ranks at three in the morning.

Amala and Pala leave message after message. They want to see the baby. Karma paces in front of the oven, clenching and unclenching her fists at her sides. A herd of elephants live next door. Their domestic battles seep through the walls in muffled surround sound.

Karma, Pema says. Maybe you could—

It's nothing to do with you, Karma snaps. Stay out of it.

But when the phone rings, Karma answers and hands Pema the other extension.

You can't come here, Karma says immediately, before their parents can say hello. Not yet.

But, Karma, Amala says. We want to help.

He doesn't want us there, Pala says. Is that the problem?

He. Pema is warming a bottle for the baby. She tests the milk against her wrist and winces.

My *husband* has a name.

Pema's parents and her sister are like warring nations, old foes skirmishing over a boundary line that shifts imperceptibly, never gaining any ground. What they need is a mediator, someone to broker a peace agreement.

Pema unscrews the nipple off the bottle and tries to think of a neutral topic. For a decade, it was just the three of them. By the time Pema arrived, the unexpected child, there was no place for a fourth party in the fray.

Amala asks about the baby. She calls her Tenzin Dolma.

Her name is Sophia, Karma says.

Pema is surprised. When had this been decided?

Tenzin Dolma. Pala speaks with authority. This name will bring her good fortune.

Were you in labour for sixteen hours? Karma's voice jumps up. Her name is Sophia Naomi Wilson.

Naomi is Jamal's mother's name. Pema puts the open bottle in the fridge and says nothing. *She* is not Ban Ki-moon. She's just the babysitter.

It's bad luck, Karma, Amala says. To reject the name Kundun has given.

Karma has no patience for superstition. I'll risk it.

Don't you want . . . we just want the baby to have the best possible chance.

Pema thinks her mother sounds frightened. She is about to speak up, but her father gets there first. Your daughter must have a Tibetan name or she will have no identity. She will be confused all her life.

She's only half Tibetan anyway, Karma says. Half Tib. Half bonobo.

Pema wants to say to her parents: Karma is having a bad day. But loyalty holds her tongue. When the call ends, Karma cries, inconsolable. Pema feels like the last sane person on earth.

A march is planned. From Queen Street to the Chinese consulate.

Karma says she is wasting her time. What's the point? Of any of this? China has won. We need to move on.

How can you say that?

If China frees Tibet, will you move there?

That's our homeland, Pema says.

On the screen Lhasa looks ravaged and desolate. An old film set, abandoned.

Some homeland, Karma says and leaves the room.

The baby tries to suckle at Pema's chest. Her shirt is damp.

At the rally, Pema is part of the crowd streaming four abreast down the street. Everything is grey and drippy. A river of melted snow runs into the gutter. Last season's rubbish—candy wrappers, cigarette butts—float past. The monks lead the way, their robes wrapped around them like burgundy bedsheets. There are signs and placards. Pema is surrounded by Tibetans. Her earliest memory: weaving in and out through a forest of legs, flitting a paper flag over her head.

The older women wear multicoloured chubas and white silk scarves. A woman in a fur-lined hat reminds Pema of her mother. The young people have painted faces. Before leaving for the rally, she had pulled down the flag that hangs in her window and now it is draped over her shoulders. There is a guy in a tricolour sweater vest with chains across his chest. She sizes him up. He's about her age and not bad-looking but there's too much gel in his hair.

A man with a bullhorn leads the chants. China lies, people die, they yell. And: One dream, one world, free Tibet! Pema walks beside an old man. He grabs her hand and squeezes as they shout together. Pema squeezes back. She wants to hug him. She feels elation and shared purpose, a sense of belonging surrounded by all these people who look just like her. She should have talked Karma into coming. They could have brought Sophia. Pema can't think of the last time Karma left the house. She must be going stir-crazy; that's her problem.

———

Brenda doesn't think self-immolation is an effective form of protest.

Amanda says it's better than suicide bombing. What other choice do they have?

It's Jamaican-me-crazy day in the cafeteria. The whole place smells like deep frying and jerk spice. Ling-Mei pulls the crust off her sandwich in one long peel.

When Pema thinks of the woman she imagines a Fanta bottle. Liquid pouring over her head, pooling like rain water in her shoes. Her teeth are barred. She lights up like a match.

Brenda is a cynic. Nothing will change.

Pema is only half-listening to the conversation. It's in the background with the cutlery and the steel pan. A thought, unguarded, makes its escape. I hate the Chinese!

Ling-Mei puts down her sandwich. Excuse me? Amanda is sitting beside Pema. She shifts away. Pema's heart beats a little faster. She has turned the corner and stumbled upon this conversation by accident and now it is too late to back away unnoticed. Her face feels hot. The Chinese government, she says.

Ling-Mei leans across the table. There is dirt under her nail. You hate the Chinese?

That's not what I meant, Pema says. Was it? Was it what she meant? She tries to explain: If they would just give us back our homeland . . . the censorship . . .

You hate the Chinese. You said it. Now stand by it.

Ling-Mei looks ready to launch herself across the table. Pema leans back. A group of old white men in crocheted rasta caps turn to watch.

Brenda puts a hand on Ling-Mei's shoulder. Pema, she says. I think you should apologize.

Amanda looks at her watch. It's time to go back.

Pema works quietly at her desk and tries not to look at Ling-Mei, who shares her cubicle. They sit with their backs to each other, clacking at their keyboards. Pema tells herself she does not hate Ling-Mei. Ling-Mei has nothing to do with inflation in Lhasa. Ling-Mei wasn't the one who beat Pala's parents to death. Ling-Mei does not know where the Panchen Lama is hidden. Pema wants to go home and hold Sophia.

At four ten the elevator doors split open. The manager of human resources is so big she needs a cane to walk. Pema has never seen her on the first floor before. She pretends to work, typing nonsense numbers into cells and staring at the computer. Has Ling-Mei said something?

The HR manager passes by Pema but stops in their cubicle. Pema tries to eavesdrop but hears only sibilant esses. Chair wheels drag backward across the carpet and then Ling-Mei and two others are following the cane to the elevator.

Pema deletes the row of numbers she has just typed and starts again. Her Dilbert calendar, the carpet-like texture of the half-wall where it hangs. Filing cabinets, inter-office envelopes, the rough shine of the key that sticks out of the drawer under her desk. All the drab grey things that surround her every day have been made unfamiliar. Pema waits and waits, but Ling-Mei does not come back.

The subway chime announces the stops in three dull tones like an unfinished melody. Pema wonders how Ling-Mei can afford to live in the Annex. When she had asked her boss, her fingers tangling and untangling, if she should be worried about the cutbacks, he'd said, You? You don't make enough money to worry. Then he'd given her Ling-Mei's files and told her: These are priority.

The balconies on the fifth floor of Ling-Mei's building jut out several inches, like a pouting lower lip. Pema has not told anyone about this visit. Something could happen and no one would know.

The wind turns her umbrella inside out. She struggles with it and follows a man with a stroller through the front door. At apartment 507 she knocks, feeling nervous. The elevator door is still open. She could jump back in, frantically press at all the buttons.

Ling-Mei wears jeans and a sweater. It's a quarter to six. If Pema was unemployed she'd still be in her pyjamas.

What are you doing here? The question is more bewildered than accusatory.

It occurs to Pema that she should have prepared a statement. What is she doing here?

Come in, Ling-Mei says, finally.

She does not offer Pema a drink or a seat. Pema doesn't unbutton her raincoat.

The office is a gong show, Pema says. I can't believe they let you go.

Ling-Mei stands with her arms crossed in front of her, all her weight cocked on one hip. She doesn't say anything and Pema feels compelled to throw a blanket over the silence: I wanted to explain about the other day, about what I said at lunch.

So explain.

Ling-Mei, so confident and sure of herself. Can she see that Pema's hands are trembling?

Pema says: The thing is . . . I'm sensitive about China.

You're sensitive about China?

I'm not explaining properly. Pema begins to sweat. Look, China . . . the Chinese government has done terrible things to us.

Ling-Mei has an underbite that gives her the look of a piranha. She says, You know I don't have anything to do with that, right? I haven't even given it much thought. China and Tibet. Who's right or wrong.

It seems to Pema a privileged position to be in—the luxury of ignorance. She says: You'd be angry too if it was your culture under threat, your family. My grandparents were beaten to death for nothing. For being in the wrong place.

It's pretty unfair of you to lump us all in together. Ling-Mei puts her hands on her hips. I wasn't even born there.

Pema is flustered. The armpits of her white button-up shirt are uncomfortably wet.

I meant the Chinese government, not the people. Not you.

Right. That's why you put those *Free Tibet* stickers on my side of the cubicle.

Pema's voice comes out louder than she intended. Are you kidding me? What about Yingying?

The Olympic mascot? Ling-Mei's arms turn cartwheels. So now I'm not allowed to keep a stuffed toy?

It's a Tibetan antelope. Pema uses her finger as an exclamation point, jabbing at Ling-Mei's nose. Which China appropriated. Because that's what you Chinese are good at—

You Chinese, you Chinese. Ling-Mei is a high-pitched parrot. We're all the same to you, aren't we, Pema?

Their voices rise, arguments clambering over each other

to come out on top. Sheets of rain slam sideways against the windows. Pema's heart is a percussionist beating in her ears.

Take responsibility for your actions! Ling-Mei stamps her foot. It's so easy to play the victim!

Ling-Mei's face grows large in Pema's vision: her dark slitted eyes, the snub petulant nose. The flat of Pema's hand winds back and swings forward, landing with a crack on Ling-Mei's cheek. Nails graze eyelash. Ling-Mei yelps and cowers, hands over her face.

Pema realizes she is breathing hard. The room comes back into focus. Ling-Mei's shoulders jerk up and for a split second, Pema thinks she's about to laugh. The piranha lip trembles. Ling-Mei wails, Why did you come here?

The sight of Ling-Mei, shattered and sobbing, is so foreign that Pema doesn't know what to make of it. She starts to cry too.

Ling-Mei presses her hands, hot and hard, into Pema's forearms and screams: GET OUT.

Pema stumbles back and somehow out the door. In the hallway, the elevator is waiting. She jabs *L* for lobby again and again and again.

At home, Pema is still thinking about Ling-Mei. She leaves the mangled umbrella on the rubber mat and recalls everything they said to each other, cringing at the memories. The way Ling-Mei's face had crumpled, her vulnerability. Pema has never raised a hand to anyone in her life. Even now she can hear the startling sound of the smack.

The TV has been left on. Victor Newman's cratered face dominates the screen. In the kitchen, two pieces of toast stand upright, golden brown. The marmalade jar is open, a knife balanced on top. When Pema touches the toaster, the stainless steel is cold.

Moving through the silent, empty rooms, Pema has the sensation of being an intruder. The unwitting neighbour who discovers the bodies.

Karm? Pema calls her sister's name softly. Fear is a tiny seed in her stomach. It might yet blow away, without taking root. From above, an odd sound, not quite like the dripping of a forgotten tap. She holds on to the banister and tells herself: Nothing is wrong. Nothing is wrong. Nothing is wrong.

The staircase is a battlefield. Soothers and burp cloths and a plush menagerie of fallen heroes. On the second floor, the bathroom sits quiet and innocent. She takes the stairs to the attic two at a time, listening hard for a cry. Instead there is singing.

She turns the corner and there's her big sister. Water slicks her hair. At her feet, the carpet darkens in a widening circle. Sophia is in her arms. The dog is close by, out of the spray, paws around his nose. When he sees Pema, he stands and barks.

Karma! What are you doing? She holds her arms out but Karma keeps Sophia to herself.

Karma sings: Just singing in the rain!

Jamal's contraption has failed. The leaky patch of ceiling has spread and the makeshift indoor plumbing cannot contain it. Pudgy bare feet hang from the bottom of a yellow raincoat. Sophia's hood is pulled up and Pema cannot see her face. The dog thumps his tail against the floor as Karma belts it out.

Drops of water dot the wall. They fleck the prayer table and fall into the bowls, rippling like rain on a pond.

Where's the bucket? Pema asks, looking around. We need towels and the roofer and . . . shut up, Fatty!

A thought stops her cold: There's no way Sophia is asleep. Not with this racket.

Karma, Pema says. What did you do?

Karma does a body sway, bobbing the baby and her shoulders. Her eyes are closed. She hums a bar wordlessly. How does the rest of the song go?

There is a little sock on the ground, pink with white frills. In the drama with Ling-Mei, Pema has forgotten her sister. Pema starts to cry. This is all her fault.

Pema says, I've done something bad.

Karma opens her eyes. She becomes still. Has something happened? Is someone hurt?

The dog begins to whine, a plaintive sound. The baby hangs in Karma's arms, unmoving.

A girl I used to . . . Pema cries harder, gasping out the words between her sobs. We got into a fight and I just . . . I slapped her.

Karma bursts out laughing. That's it? she says between guffaws. You bitch-slapped some chick and that's why you're crying? She puts a hand on Pema's shoulder. Pema. Relax. You'll apologize. I'll call the roofer. Your friend will live. The carpet will survive. Now do you know the words to this song or what?

Karma's laugh—loud, almost masculine—Pema hasn't heard it in weeks. She shakes her head. Or what, she says.

My god! Karma says. The look on your face . . . I thought someone had . . . Come here. Karma pulls her under the leak. Feel this. It's not cold.

Pema sees that Karma is smiling, for the first time in a long time. And closer now, she sees that, incredibly, Sophia *is* asleep, snuffly breaths puffing out. The carpet is a sponge and then so are Pema's socks.

Here's a song I know. Pema thinks for a second, recalling the right key. It's raining men!

Pema puts her arms around Karma and with Sophia a sleeping bundle between them, they sing, dancing in a circle. Hair glues itself to Pema's cheek. Water anoints her head, tickling down the back of her neck, under her shirt. The warmth of Karma's body. The sour odour of sweat and breast milk. But none of it matters. Because they are both singing. Madly, joyously. Elephants stamping down the stairs. Turning and turning. Faster, faster. A trinity spinning like a prayer wheel. The walls, the colours of the thangka, everything blurring. Rain pelts the roof. Fatty howls. Pema and her sister shout: Amen! Karma laughs and the baby wakes up with a yawn.

MICHAEL MEAGHER

USED TO IT

We wash and dry those big entrance mats you see slopped down inside offices and government buildings and banks. Our guys drive all over the city in cube vans, picking up those dirty mats before backing up to the bay doors. From the outside, the warehouse looks like a giant storage shed. Rusty, corrugated sheets of steel gunned into concrete. The floor's grey and cracked, and there must be a million clean mats stacked neatly on shelves. Row after row after row. Waiting to be taken away. Rubber, carpet, studded, 6' x 8', 6' x 10', 8' x 10', 10' x 12'. They all have their proper place among the barrels of chemicals and cleaning solvents.

A couple guys unload the vans, and one runs the washers, and another the dryers. When a dryer bell rings, two buttons are pressed—the first tilts the hulking machine forward, the second spins the mats into a twisted mess, spitting them onto a cart in the process. I dabble a bit, but mostly untangle. Imagine trying to straighten out a boxspring-sized pretzel made of rubber. Then doing it a hundred times. Heaving and jerking like a turtle on its back. The final—and easiest—step is folding and stacking the mats.

Before my hands hardened and withered like sun-dried tomatoes, the heat in the rubber would burn into them. Eat right through the Kevlar gloves. The work's messed up the rest of my body too. I'm only thirty, but you'd probably guess forty, or maybe even fifty. A lifetime of steam and cancer in ten years. Battery acid seeping into all the folds and cracks of skin. My face and arms bumpy like a gourd or avocado rind. Although I'm well set and you'd be hard-pressed to find a roll of fat, you might say I've become ugly, or, at the very least, an acquired taste.

My shift runs noon till ten or eleven. Sometimes longer. That means a good piece of overtime with each paycheque. The idea of an extra couple hundred bucks every two weeks was nice in the beginning, but it quickly became an expectation, so it's not so special after all.

Me and Simms are always the last to take off. He runs the final loads, and I work apart the mats. "Grab the knot and tug," he said once. "If it doesn't work, go to the other side of the cart, try another angle. You always wanna be moving, always bucking. Like a bull. Never flatfooted. Remember that," he said, "'cause I won't tell you again."

Jonathan Skidmore was on the job only three days. The work seemed simple enough: pour the chemical from a larger container into a smaller one. The supplier label identified this chemical as flammable and combustible. Jonathan knew that flammable and combustible means more than simply not smoking in the area. You also have to make sure that there is no equipment nearby creating sparks, flames, or heat, and to take precautions to prevent the buildup of static electricity.

Jonathan walked over to the larger container and removed the cap. Without warning, the chemical burst into flames.

The fire burned 80 per cent of Jonathan's body.

How could this senseless tragedy have been prevented?

Jonathan's employer should have told him that certain liquids may cause static electricity to build up while they are being poured.

The fire that burned Jonathan was started by static electricity.

To prevent static electricity from building up you must ground the larger container to a ground in the building, then you must bond the larger container you are pouring from to the smaller container you are pouring into.

Jonathan died three days later in the hospital.

The instructor got out of his chair and walked to the front of the room, where he'd been standing before the video started. He'd dabbed himself with cologne that morning, so he stunk of iodine and spruce. He wore a polo shirt with an insignia on the shoulder. A tiny knight's helmet. Probably the mascot of the business school he graduated from. In the chest pocket, he'd tucked three pens. One each of black, blue, and red. He wore creased khakis and a pair of dress shoes. Didn't look a day over twenty, although it's hard to tell with men like him. Men who don't work with their bodies.

The old guy, Art, would wear jeans and a STIHL or John Deere sweatshirt. And he never stood while he talked. He'd sit at the table with everyone while explaining how to clean a chemical spill. Then he'd take a stack of laminated pictures out of his binder. "This is the sign for flammable," he'd say, holding up a picture of what looked like a Boy Scout's campfire.

"And believe it or not," he'd laugh, grabbing another sheet from the pile, a drawing of a test tube or thermometer shaped like a condom, "this still means compressed gas."

He'd turn off the lights for the video, to make the experience more cinematic. And when he related back to case studies of guys whiffing unlabelled chemicals, he'd look at us with this puzzled expression that meant *what fucking idiots*. The new guy was all business, though. He even put clinical photos on the overhead. Arms covered in blood blisters, a pussing eye socket the size of a grapefruit.

"Did anyone take notes?" he said. "That's why I keep the lights on during training videos."

"No one took fucking notes," Simms said.

"Easy, Charlie," Tony said. "He's just doing his job."

"Just give me the fucking test."

Charlie Simms has been working the washers for a couple decades. Right out of high school, I've been told. But his skin isn't droopy like some of ours. It clings to his face like plastic wrap. Like he's been given Botox injections. So perfect it's off-putting. I'm sure that's why Tony, the manager, hasn't canned Simms—who knows what demented cells are pulsing inside, and if he's capable of charging into the warehouse with a shotgun.

"It's all right," the instructor said. "I'll be out of your hair soon."

After he handed out the tests, he pressed a button on his watch and said, "You have twenty minutes."

He walked to the head of the table and crossed his arms in front of his chest. He hadn't been bothered by Simms— this wasn't the first time a grown man had cursed at him—but the instructor still looked like a schoolboy watching a tennis match.

Maybe the test was always meant to be twenty minutes, but Art was laidback. He'd give out the tests and tell everyone to take their time, then leave the room. Go to the bathroom or down the street for a coffee. He'd knock before coming back. "Hope nobody cheated," he'd joke.

What should you do if you spot an unknown liquid on the ground? A. Taste it to see what it is B. Smell it to see what it is C. Consult your supervisor immediately D. Put on gloves and wipe it up. Nothing differed from previous years. Questions, right answers, wrong answers. Even though Art was gone, I was relieved—maybe we all were—because the whole operation hadn't changed.

There are white collars like Tony. Older guys whose work has started to catch up with them. It's happened right in front of my eyes. You can't see it at first because it's deep inside. Then one day you notice a grey moustache hair or a widow's peak receding. A step that's lost its spring. Before you know it, sick leave. Ulcers and migraine headaches. I've never worked an office job, but I've seen people come and go.

And then there are white collars like that young instructor. And like Adam, the guy who'd been hired on as the new secretary. Adam's face was clean and pale and his hair always combed to the side. Poking out the sleeves of his button-down, his hands were white and chalky as latex gloves. He reminded me of a fawn being exposed to the ugliness of the world for the first time. So cute you want to kiss or snap its neck.

It was on the bench outside the warehouse I first talked to

Adam. Right after the training video. I'd just tapped a cigarette on the pack a few times and brought it to my lips.

"I always see people do that," he said, sitting beside me.

"Do what?" I said.

"Tap their cigarettes. I've never known why."

"Me neither."

We sat there for a minute, looking out at the field. It wasn't
winter yet but most of the weedy grasses had already died
back. It was only in late spring and summer they looked
almost alive. A couple months later the field would be hard
with ice, and the garden plants on the warehouse-side of the
chain-link fence flattened out and yellow.

"Do you have an extra one of those?" Adam pointed to the
pack of cigarettes lying on the bench between us.

"Go ahead."

He took one out of the pack and put it to his lips. "Do you
mind? It's the wind," he said. He shielded the cigarette with
his hands while I flicked the lighter.

"Thanks. I'm Adam, by the way."

"Tom." We reached out to shake hands. Me with my fat
parsnip fingers and him with his hairless, pencil-thin ones. By
his grip, you knew he was a typist or a secretary, and couldn't
have handled a day or even an hour downstairs. Steam and
boiling water and splintered backs and anger. Packed together
like wet clay and chucked into the corner of the warehouse.
The Pit, it's called.

"How long have you worked here, Tom?"

"Long enough, anyways."

"I should've been looking at your test, then," he said, laughing smoke out his mouth.

"That may not have helped."

"So where do you put the butts?" He held out the half-smoked cigarette.

"Just anywhere."

He dropped it on the ground, twisted it out with his foot.

"Thanks for the smoke," he said, then got up and brushed off the front of his pants.

I'd come out of the bathroom wearing my new uniform. Navy blue work pants and a white T-shirt. "They're a little tight," I said to Tony.

"You'll grow into them in no time. It's like a sauna down here," he said. "In a good way."

"Whatever you say."

"Great," Tony said, clapping his hands together. "Charlie here will show you everything."

There were three dryers side by side. Each as big as an upright minivan. At a right angle to the row of dryers were three washers. The machines formed an L, and gave a sense of enclosure. At the near side of the dryers was an open space with a large table. This is where Charlie Simms took me. Wheeling a cart of hot, tangled mats behind.

"Watch closely" were the first words that left his mouth. While Tony had talked, Simms just stood there, eyeballing. Trying to think of one good reason not to go batshit crazy and scare me away.

Simms bent his knees and clasped one of those rubber mats. He jerked his legs straight while tugging with his arms. He tugged again and again. Like a shock absorber having a seizure. When he finally yanked out the mat, like a tooth, he slopped it on the table. "If it's not working," he said, "get angry. Anger's your friend here."

"What am I doing exactly?" I asked.

"What I just did there," he said. "And when the mats pile up on the table, fold 'em and put 'em away. Now get to work."

Partway to the washing station, he looked over his shoulder. He saw the dumb look on my face and came right back to where I was standing. "What the fuck did I say? Start ripping those things apart or you're finished. You hear me?"

With most jobs, there's that awkward first moment—even if it's only a minute or two—where you get your instructions, where you look at one of the old-timers and try to follow what they're doing. But at a warehouse, there was no real first moment, no moment that lay somewhere between working and not working.

The door was opened. And as it closed, I heard the bristles along the bottom sweep across the concrete. Then the scuff of dress shoes as Adam came to the bench. He bent over beside me and put down an empty can of tomato sauce.

"For the butts," he said, sitting down. "Do you mind if I have a cigarette?" he said, slipping a few quarters out of his pocket.

"It's all right," I said. "Go ahead."

"Are you the only one who smokes around here?"

"No, a couple of the other guys do."

"And where are they?"

"I guess if we all took break at the same time, we'd fall behind."

"So what's it like working downstairs?"

"Well. We clean the mats and then we dry and fold the mats. That's all there is to it. And before that, we unload them from the cube vans."

"It must keep you in shape, at least. Maybe not like pushing pens all day, though," he said, laughing while pretending to flex his biceps muscle.

A noise left the back of my throat, halfway between a huh and a laugh. "Probably nothing like that," I said.

A guy came into the lunch room an hour into his first shift. "I messed my back up some good," he said to me. He was hunched over and reaching around, squeezing his lower back with his hands.

"Then take a seat," I said. "Drink some water."

Simms stormed into the room and put his nose in the new guy's face like he was acting out some sort of mating ritual. "Get the fuck back out there," Simms said.

"I think I threw my back out, boss."

"I don't care what you did. We're falling behind. I'm gonna see you in the Pit in thirty seconds," Simms said, then left. I'll tell you now that Simms doesn't discriminate. What I mean is that nobody's off the hook. It's fuck this and faggot that with everyone. His own mother could snap her arm in half and Simms wouldn't feel bad.

"I don't know about this, pal," the new guy said to me. "I've done my share of construction over the years, but nothing like this. No, not like this."

"You have about fifteen seconds to decide," I said, pointing at the wall clock.

Just as the new guy's lips touched the arc of water spurting out the fountain, Simms came in. "What the fuck did I tell you?"

"It's my back, boss," the new guy said.

"Stop being such a pussy and get out there."

"I think I'm finished."

"When are you off break? Five minutes?" Simms said to me.

"I looked at the clock. "Seven."

"Fuck."

Simms walked out the lunch room and the new guy out the front door. I once saw a guy quit after ten minutes. "Tell your boss 'thanks but no thanks.' This work isn't for me," he said. Walking off. Something I should've done by now. Before getting on at the warehouse, I'd jumped around for a couple years. Dishwashing, food prep, mopping floors. It was easier to leave those jobs. Sure, I was younger. But I also hadn't had a ten-year habit in my system.

"Mind if I have a drag?" Adam said.

"You can just take one," I said and grabbed the cigarettes from the bench.

"I never smoke a whole one, anyways."

"I guess not." I blew smoke out the side of my mouth and passed him the cigarette.

He brought it to his lips and inhaled. He took another drag, then passed it back, a smear of saliva across the filter. "Sorry about that," he said.

"I don't mind." I brought the cigarette to my mouth, and my lips covered the smudge. It tasted sweet. Like honey or jasmine. Kissing him flashed through my head. Then jamming my dick down his throat. Those lips. Soft as applesauce.

That's what happens when you go so long without touching someone—things pop into your head from nowhere.

I blew the smoke out my mouth, then took one last drag before dropping it in the tomato can beside the bench. It was just a blotch of glue keeping the label attached.

I lit another cigarette and gave it to Adam. After he inhaled the smoke, he rested his arm on his knee, the cigarette dangling between his limp fingers.

"How's it going downstairs?" he asked, giving me the cigarette.

"We had a new guy in there this afternoon."

"How's he doing?"

"I don't think he's coming back."

"No?"

"He couldn't relax, is all. The thing is, no matter what you do, the mats keep piling up."

"So what happened?"

"The usual story. It was his back. And Simms."

"Simms," he repeated, as if turning the world over in his head.

"I guess there's nothing you can do, though." I took a long drag and looked across the frozen field. I took another, passed Adam the cigarette. "And how's it going upstairs, then?"

"The same as downstairs, probably, except that it's paper, and there was no new guy," he said, laughing.

We sat there for a minute. I looked out at the icy field and Adam stared at the ground between his feet.

"So what's the deal with Charlie?" he said.

"You mean Simms? He's a piece of shit is what's the deal with him."

"'Cause he calls me gay whenever he sees me. Nearly every day for the past two months."

"You mean he calls you faggot?"

"Right."

"And are you?"

"Of course not."

"Then I wouldn't go around feeling special about it. He's called me faggot for ten years, along with everyone else. If it's not that, it's fuck face or shit hole or pussy."

"Isn't there something we can do?"

"Not really," I said. "I'd tell you he's still around because he's loyal. And because he's a good worker. But that would be horseshit. Between you and me, I think Tony's scared of him."

"Really?"

"Maybe. I don't see what else it could be."

"Jesus," he said. "And it's just the two of you every night?"

"For the last couple hours."

"How do you do it?"

"I ignore him. And that's what you should do."

"Still. Be careful, Tom."

"I'd worry about yourself."

Barney's teeth are bucked and crooked, and his mouth's always half open. Like he's on the verge of talking. And his face sags like he's got weights hooked into the cheeks. His shoulders are sloped and he's a little bent over. As if he's constantly about to grab something off the ground. He goes fast but doesn't run. Or even walk. He shuffles with varying degrees of speed. Loading one dryer, unloading the next. Rolling carts of spun-up mats to the folding table.

By the time I start shift, he's been running the dryers for an hour. And there's a line of carts waiting for me. We've worked together a few years, but I couldn't tell you much about him. If we're lucky, I have time to say, "Hey, Barney," and he says, "Hey, bud," and the afternoon starts off on the right foot. Otherwise, Simms tells us we're not paid to *fucking* socialize before Barney can get a word in. So I grab one of the knots of hot rubber and tug, feel the blood rush into my crapped-out back. And Barney slouches over to the machines, ready for eight or nine or ten more hours of steam and vinegar and bleach. Screaming into his eyes and palms and gums like a shattered windshield.

Sometimes I'm on a roll. Yanking mats out of the rubber snarl, flopping them onto the folding table. Like I have a gift. But sooner or later, Barney brings a lump of mats that ruins my rhythm. Even if the mind's still game, the body won't co-operate. It's irrational, but in these moments I resent Barney. He seems like a decent guy, but I want to shove his face into a vat of antifreeze.

On top of the three regulars—Barney, me, and Simms—and the guys driving and unpacking the vans, there's a drifter. A guy who works wherever he's needed. Untangling, folding, shelving. He might last a day or a week. Or half an hour. For that, he can thank the muscles and joints in his back. Shutting down before toughening up. He can also thank his hands. Covered in blisters and boils, some of them bloody. And it's not just the heat and friction. It's the rubber studs on the mat bottoms. A thousand thumbtacks chewing across twisting palms.

This guy—the drifter—rarely straightens out a cart in under ten minutes. But someone whose hands have been burnt numb, who's okay with gripping a tar-hot mat and wrenching, not letting go till it's free—someone like me—can tackle a load in six or seven minutes. Once or twice—and only once or twice—I may've gone down to five minutes. If I ever did four minutes, Simms would cry to management. "We gotta knock thirty seconds off the dryers," he'd say. "To keep him on his toes." That's because a dry cycle's twelve minutes, and there are three dryers. Which means every four minutes, Barney wheels over a cart.

My back and hands may be hardened, but I've never gotten used to the bells. A buzzer means something's ready, but a bell means something needs to be done. A dryer bell clangs every four minutes, which is fifteen bells an hour. In a twelve-hour shift, 180 emergencies. And double that with the washing machines. No matter how far ahead you are, you're always on edge. Like trying to sleep under a smoke alarm with a low battery.

Bells take the place of familiar things—sun, moon, flower bud, nut sack, nipple. Naked men are in line. Marching beside a staggered row. Pyramid cedars and drying machines. One of the men is Adam. A bow tied around the base of his erection, his balls jingling. He tries to say something, but he's got a dinner bell for a face. So a metallic screech comes out. A bolt shot into my eardrum. Waking up wet. I sit, make for the lump of tangled rubber beside the folding table. But I stop and go back to bed. The people in those banks and office buildings don't know about this. Or that I even exist. A mat's taken away, another's slopped down. If my body hadn't been cut out for the warehouse—if I were a drifter—maybe I'd have gone to college. And become a filer. Hiding behind staples and pencils and stacks of paper by day. Cold sweating over them by night.

———

Adam was already sitting on the bench, which meant something wasn't right. He was looking at the field, all its grasses soggy from the spring rain.

I sat down, then lit a cigarette and passed it over.

"I'll see if I can't quit once and for all," he said. "A fresh start."

"What's wrong?"

"Today's my last day," he said. "I wanted to tell you sooner but couldn't. I don't know why."

I took a drag, then dropped the cigarette in the can. The label that said tomato sauce was gone. The wind and rain had been sneaking under, peeling the strip of paper from the steel. I don't know how many times I've walked over to the green garbage container and dumped a full can of butts. I never get them all out, though. Some always cling to the bottom. Wet and brown and permanent.

"I don't think I've ever seen you leave a cigarette unfinished," Adam said.

I've spent my warehouse years losing touch with everyone I know. At first, I'd still go out on weekends. I was proud of my thick arms and think fingers. Stained with sweat and solvent. Dark as tobacco juice. I'd even bring the odd guy back to my apartment. Put my seven inches to good use. But I changed with time. And could never sleep enough. Then Adam came along.

"It's funny," I said. "How you get used to it. A job, looking out at a field, sharing a cigarette on a bench."

"Have you ever thought about leaving?" he said.

"I've thought about a lot of things."

"No. Seriously."

I squinted at the clump of maples at the far end of the field. Short and fat. Like candy apples stuck in mud. "Did Simms have something to do with this?" I said.

"With me leaving?" he said. "I wouldn't say that, but just thinking of him gives me the creeps. I had a dream a while back. I'm working upstairs as usual. Everything looks fine, except I'm alone. I hear someone walking up the stairs. Turns out it's Simms. He stands there, pointing a gun at me. Just as he's about to pull the trigger, I wake up. And I never even worked with him."

"So it's because of Simms?"

"I never liked it here. The money, the hours, the work. None of it. Except you."

"Let me talk to him."

"There's no use. You said so yourself. Besides, even if he had something to do with this, it's too late."

"I guess you got a job lined up, then?"

"Yeah," he said. "It pays well."

"Maybe I can go work with you."

"A couple clerks riding off into the sunset together," he laughed.

"That would be the day, wouldn't it?"

"Let's go for a drink sometime, though. Here's my number," he said, handing me a piece of paper. "I should get going, but call me." He put his hands on his thighs, then sat up from the bench. He patted my back and headed for the door.

I went with Adam the other day. This bar on the other side of the city. "I came here in university," he told me. Oak tables and oak chairs and oak countertop. Glazed and cloudy.

Mozzarella sticks and fries and nacho cheese bubbling behind swinging doors. The place was divey enough that Adam could squeeze the inside of my leg under the table, slide his hand up the denim. But not so divey that he couldn't have his red wine.

He had his little boy's haircut and his collared shirt. But he drank, all right. Until we stood and walked past the table of college kids. Past the neighbourhood men slouched over the counter. So shrivelled they'd be wasted—although you wouldn't know—off a single pint. Paid the tab and fell into my car. Drove to my place. "Because I have roommates," he said. His hand on the back of my neck, the other down the front of my pants. My hands on the steering wheel. Raining outside. The red and green and yellow lights like slits. Then fumbling for the apartment key and teasing it into the key hole. Kitchen with a toaster oven, microwave, and a buzzing fridge. Dishes teetering in the sink. A mattress, and a television on a stand. Grey carpet. Musty like maggots on compost. And we're both naked, lying in bed. He's how I imagined. Chest flat as plywood. Just enough ass to grab on to. Nipples the size of fly bites. "It's been a while," I say. But no words behind his wine-pink teeth. Just his lips on my neck. Wet bodies slow. And then fast. Like mats being slapped together.

The white collars clear out. Then it's the guys driving and unpacking the cube vans. Then Barney. That leaves me and Simms. He's whipping the last of those sandy mats through the machines, and I'm working the folding table. I wait a good fifteen minutes after Barney leaves, then walk across the Pit, right up to Simms. "What the fuck are you doing, faggot? If we wanna be outta here by next week, get the fuck back over there," he says, pointing to the backlog of bloated carts beside the dryers.

"I'm gay, Simms," I say.

"I know. Why don't you unplug your fucking ears?"

"You're not hearing me," I say.

I'd planned on Simms going wild. But after skipping a beat. Trying to understand what I'd told him. It was in this confused moment that I'd hoof him between the legs. Watch him drop to the concrete. Squirm there like a beetle. I'd roll him onto his back, press my foot into his sternum.

"Look at me," I'd say, but he'd wince.

"And this one's for Adam," I'd say, belting him a second time in the nuts. And one last shot—a bent-over haymaker—to the nose. Just to see him bleed. My wallet and keys and cigarettes would be in my pockets, but I'd leave everything else behind. Jacket, street clothes, backpack. Scrunched at the bottom of my locker. He'd be worming around like burning Jonathan Skidmore. And I'd book it to the car and twist the key in the ignition. Blaze home. "Come with me," I'd tell Adam. "Just shut up and come with me." He'd say yes, and we'd drive the gas out of the tank. Hole ourselves in a motel for the night, then keep driving. He'd find another job. And so would I.

Simms looks like a boy lost in the rain. I even give him a chance to rage, to justify messing him up. But he just stands there. This boy. So I walk out the door and drive home. Go back to work the next day, because who am I kidding? I say nothing and Simms says nothing. He never does. Only pussy and fuck-o. But no more faggot. What kind of logic is that?

SARAH KABAMBA

THEY COME CRYING

"Back home, when someone dies, you can hear the women crying throughout the entire village," Baba tells me, sitting on the edge of my bed. The glow from my night light leaks into the wrinkles in his face and highlights the grey in his curly black hair.

From downstairs, I hear the crying. I can tell which cries are Mama's. They're the loudest, guttural and raw with grief. Baba continues to talk. I try to listen but all I can hear are the wails from below. Baba stops talking and looks at me expectantly. I pick at a stray thread on my flowered bedcovers.

"Ada," he says. "Are you even listening?"

I continue to pull at the frayed thread. I want to build a fort with my covers and hide there with my hands over my ears.

"Mama Dalia, your mother's sister, has died." Baba lifts my chin up with a finger, forcing me to meet his brown eyes. "Ada. I need you to go be with your mother."

I stand still as Baba wraps the bright purple and yellow patterned *kikwembe* around my waist. The cloth covers my

Care Bears pyjama pants and hangs to the floor. It's loose, Mama always ties it nice and tight so I don't trip over the edges.

"My older sister, Janie, showed me how to tie these," Baba says. He looks at me and the corner of his mouth tips up. "I never paid attention."

"Are you going to come downstairs too?" I ask.

Baba shakes his head. "Women and men don't mourn together. The men will come tomorrow."

Baba hugs me and I snuggle into his chest. The wool of his sweater tickles my cheeks. I feel his heart beating like a drum and for a moment I can almost ignore the crying coming from downstairs.

"*Nakupenda*," Baba whispers in Swahili.

"Love you too," I whisper back.

I slip out of his arms and stand at the foot of the stairs. There are fourteen steps. I count them in my head as I go down. The seventh step always creaks but tonight I don't even hear it over the weeping.

My *kikwembe* drags against the cold tile of the kitchen floor as I make my way into the living room. Mama sits on the floor in front of the fireplace surrounded by women. Their wails rise and weave with one another. I recognize Mama Jina and Mama Nuru. The other women are vaguely familiar in the way aunts and uncles that you only see on holidays are.

Mama Jina, who is beside Mama, motions me over. "*Mtoto*," she says, standing up. "Who tied this for you?" She picks at the knot Baba tied, rewraps the colourful material around my waist, and secures it at my right hip.

I sit beside Mama. She doesn't look at me. She just continues to cry and scream. She rocks back and forth, tears running down her cheeks, and the other women join in. I bow my head to hide the absence of tears from my own eyes. I want desperately to feel something but I can barely bring the image of my aunt to mind. I've never met her, only seen pictures and heard stories. She's never been real to me, just a name of a woman in Congo that my parents promised I would one day meet.

I look up and one of the women is looking at me with narrowed brows, tears glistening on her dark skin. *"Ambaye ni mtoto huyu ambaye hawezi kulia?"*

Whose is this child who doesn't cry? I keep my head bowed and pinch the skin of my arm until tears rise to the corner of my eyes.

The kitchen is full of chattering voices and brightly patterned *kikwembes.* Oil sizzles in the pan as the plantain fries, okra boils in a pot, and one of the women heats water for the *fufu* in the largest pot we have.

"You're going to burn the plantain," Mama Nuru says to no one in particular.

"Where do you keep the *piri piri?*" another woman asks me.

I take the plastic container with the ground spices out of the fridge and hand it to her. She thanks me and turns back to the stove.

"Will you make the *fufu?*" Mama Jina asks me in Swahili.

The woman who had glared at me yesterday clucks in surprise. "Oh, she speaks Swahili?"

Mama Jina shakes her head. "Not fluently, Aisha, but she understands it."

I look Mama Aisha in the eye and I wonder if she is remembering what she said last night. She meets my gaze steadily and doesn't look away. "*Utafanya?*" she challenges.

I remember all the times Mama tried to teach me to make *fufu* and how I would never really pay attention. My dough always ended up too watery or full of lumps.

I look at Mama Jina. "I don't know how," I whisper.

"*Kuja.*" Mama Jina takes my arm. "You can make the rice."

Behind me, Mama Aisha clucks again. "A shame, not being able to make *fufu* at her age."

The doorbell rings. I hear Baba's firm footsteps down the stairs. He opens the door to let the men in. They fill the foyer and speak in hushed voices as they follow Baba into his office. Bits and pieces of their conversation float into the kitchen and then one of the men pushes the door closed. The men have left their shoes in a careless pile and Mama Jina rearranges them, lining them up into pairs.

When we are done cooking, every surface of the wooden kitchen table is covered with pots and plates. The food that could not fit is crammed onto the kitchen island. We stand around the table, eyes closed, as Baba leads the prayer. When he's done, the men go sit at the dining room table in the other room, the one that we only use for special occasions and guests. The women prepare plates for their husbands. Mama Jina hands me a plate for Baba. I fill it with rice, fish, plantain, *sombe*, and *fufu*. Silently, the women slide the plates in front of the men, who do not pause in their conversation. Mama Nuru, whose husband died last year, goes around the table filling the glasses with water.

Back in the kitchen, the women now fix plates for themselves. Mama Jina hands me a full plate.

"Bring it to your mother," she says.

Mama is on the living room floor, where she has been since last night. The women who were not helping in the kitchen are sitting with her. I kneel down in front of her and present her the plate. She makes no move to take it. My knees ache and my hand trembles with the weight of the plate, but I don't move.

"*Kula*," one of the women whispers to Mama. She takes the plate from me and places it on Mama's outstretched legs.

Silently, tears roll down Mama's high cheekbones, falling on the edge of the plate, and I just stay there, knees aching.

The living room is dark. Some of the women sleep on the couch. Some on the floor. I am curled up by Mama's side with Mama Jina's *kikwembe* pulled around my shoulders. I can't see Mama's face but I can hear her tears and feel the sobs racking her body. I stretch my thin arms around her and squeeze as hard as I can.

———∽∞∽———

"Your mother has to go to Kinshasa to bury her sister," Baba says to me.

The house is temporarily empty; the women have gone home to tend to their own households and children. Only Mama Nuru, who has coaxed Mama upstairs to take a bath, remains. The kitchen tile is cold under my bare feet and I let my hands sink into the dirty dishwater.

"For how long?" I ask.

"A week at most. She's leaving tomorrow."

I don't say anything and Baba looks up from the computer, where he is buying Mama's plane ticket.

"She'll be back before you know it," he says. "I just need you to keep being a big girl for a little while longer."

⚭

Mama Nuru, Mama Jina, Mama Aisha, and all the other women come to see Mama off at the airport. They take turns hugging her and whispering reassurances into her ear. All of them cry. When it's my turn, I hug Mama as hard as I can. I open my mouth but there are no words and all I can do is squeeze her tighter.

The women come back to the house with Baba and me. They will stay until Mama Dalia is buried in Kinshasa. We clean the house. We cook. Mama Nuru and Mama Jina braid my hair with colourful beads. We clean and cook some more.

On the third day Mama's been gone, we do not cook. We do not clean. The women and I sit in silence in the living room. Nobody says anything. Every so often someone shifts or gets up to use the bathroom but otherwise nobody moves.

Mama Aisha begins to cry and suddenly they're all weeping. The room is filled with their sobs, and their sorrow suffocates me as I sit there, silent and dry-eyed. Outside, the sky goes from a golden caramel to an inky darkness broken only by the glimmer of stars. As the women continue to wail, I stare at the twinkling stars and wish that my aunt would come back and make Mama happy again.

The shrill ring of the phone breaks the rhythm of their cries. Mama Nuru answers the phone, listens, and hangs up. "*Ni kufanyika*," she announces to the room.

Like a record winding down, the women's cries slowly stutter and stop.

For the rest of the time Mama is gone, the women take turns stopping by. They stay for a bit, drop off dishes of food, and talk to Baba. Before they leave, they always hug me and ask if I'm okay. I know that they don't want to hear that I miss Mama, that I'm scared that she will never come back, so I don't say any of this.

One day while Baba is out, Mama Aisha comes by. I stare at her through the glass window of the front door. I don't want to let her in but I know I have to.

"Took you long enough," she says, handing me a casserole.

I follow her into the kitchen and set the dish on the island. I lift the lid and peek in.

"Puff-puffs!" the words leave my mouth before I can stop myself.

"Do you know how to make those?" Mama Aisha asks.

I look up from the casserole full of deep-fried doughnut balls to see a slight smile on her face.

"Mama showed me how," I reply.

"Let's make some more then. Your *baba* will finish these as soon as he gets home."

I stare at her in surprise.

"Well? Don't just stand there, get the ingredients."

As we mix the flour, sugar, eggs, and yeast, Mama Aisha begins to talk.

"My mama taught me how to make these. She would sell them in the village marketplace. Some days I would go with her."

Mama Aisha abandons the wooden spoon and begins

kneading the dough with her hands. "One day," she continues, "Mama got sick. She was too weak to even beat the dough. I had to make the puff-puffs and sell them or else we wouldn't have any money."

"Where was your *baba*?" I ask.

"He left. He had another wife." She looks down at her flour-covered hands and shakes her head.

"When Mama died, everybody in the village came. They stayed with me until her burial. They cooked for me, fed me, cried with me. And after, one of the women took me in as her own daughter."

I look up at Mama Aisha. She's stopped kneading the dough.

"Do you still miss her?" I ask.

She nods, a tear leaks out of the corner of her eye. "*Mauti hutia kilio*," she whispers.

I cock my head. Mama Aisha sniffles and smiles at me. "It's an old proverb. It means: 'Death makes people cry. One day the seriousness of life will be brought home to everyone.' One day the seriousness of life will come to you too. Now you want your mother to come home to you, and that is okay."

I don't realize that I'm crying until I see the drip of tears on the dough in front of me. Mama Aisha reaches over and wipes my face with flour-streaked fingers. "If we keep this up, our puff-puffs will be so salty that no one will eat them."

We finish making the puff-puffs and then we do the dishes. Mama Aisha hums as she dries. Before she leaves, she hugs me and tells me to greet Baba for her. Later that night, I can't sleep so I clean the house. It's not dirty. I try to erase the remnants of sorrow from the walls but I can still hear the echoes of crying no matter how much I scrub, sweep, and mop.

The women come early the next day. They come laughing. They come singing. They come with brightly coloured *kikwembes*. They come with cassava leaves, plantains, okra, *ndakala*, *piri piri*, and yams. The kitchen fills with the sound of oil sizzling as we fry the plantains and fish. Okra boils on one of the back burners. Sliced yams are piled high on the counter waiting to be boiled. Mama Nuru sifts flour for the *fufu*. As they work, the women sing, their voices weaving in and out with one another.

I sit on the floor, beating the *piri piri* in the mortar with the wooden pestle. The spices sting my eyes, and unbidden tears leak out of the corners.

Mama Aisha dances past me and says, *"Ambaye ni mtoto huyu ambaye analia wakati wengine kucheka?"*

Whose is this child who cries while others laugh? She smiles at me and I smile back.

The table is set. My hair is brushed and braided. Green and yellow beads, Mama's favourite colours, clink together at the ends of my braids. I wear her old yellow *kikwembe* with the matching top. The women talk quietly as we wait for Baba to come back home with Mama. I sit by the window and watch as cars go by. Our red Camry rolls into view and I can't move. What will I do if she's still crying? What will I do if she refuses to eat again? Will she talk now? Will she smile again? Will she—

"Mtoto," Mama Aisha says, breaking into my thoughts. *"Kwende."*

And so I go. I slip off the couch and out the door. The pavement is bumpy under my bare feet but I barely feel the rocks as I run toward Mama.

SHARON BALA

READING WEEK

A room. Seventeen by seventeen. Opposite sides like inverse images. Something like that. Outside: a knock. Soft. Uncertain. Inside: guitars, bass, drums. Late-nineties alterna-rock. Angry. Angst-ridden.

Girl at a desk. Hair, ponytailed. Or turbaned in damp towel. Doesn't matter. Plaid flannels. T-shirt, possibly frayed. Abbotsford High. Bare feet. No. Slippers. Once plush, now worn. Pencil. Tap, tap, tap against textbook. Bits of twisted rubber, eraser crumbs everywhere. Goosenecked lamp.

Another knock. Louder. Nine steps to the door. Distracted. Product Rule $(fg)' = f'g + fg'$. Pencil clamped in mouth. Teeth bared. Door swings inward.

Now, everything in slow motion.

At first Jo doesn't recognize him. His flecked, green eyes, the turning down at the mouth, the scar under his left ear. Who is this guy standing expectantly in the doorway of her room? She takes her pencil out of her mouth, ready to ask. But then the stranger sinks his fingers into his hair and it is Jeremy.

All these years he's remained frozen in her imagination: sixteen, a child on the cliff's edge of adulthood. Two years ago, she had vaulted past him.

Grocery store cake. Carrot, her least favourite. Seventeen candles. Pink wax dripping. Cream cheese frosting. Inside of eyelids: orange and black. Make a wish. Exhale. Hard. Now, here it is: her wish come true. Seventh time. Charm. Etc.

"Hi." They speak in unison, two sides of the same voice—male and female.

All the things she wants to say occur to her at once: What are you doing here / Where have you been / Are you okay / Do you have any idea.

"How's it going?" This. This was what she has chosen to say.

"Can I come in?"

How long has she been standing here, mouth like a guppy? "Uh yeah. Sorry. Of course. Sure." She steps aside and then her brother is in her room.

More things Jo wants to say: Oh my God / Do Mom and Dad know / Stay.

"Cool room. Nice tree."

"That belongs to Alice." Jo steps around the stump and waves her hand around the far side of the room. "This is my half." She presses a button. Radio silence.

"I like them too." He points to her CD player with his chin.

The conversation is too normal. Jo wants to dial back three beats. "How did you find me?" Finally, a real question.

"I saw you. On Princess Street."

"You live here?"

"No. I'm going to Montreal. A guy in a pickup dropped me off."

"And then you saw me."

"I wasn't sure. Not right away."

Jo tries to work it out. She had gone to the A&P for Kraft Dinner and Jeremy had followed her home. "But I've been here since seven."

He doesn't respond and she doesn't really notice. Because she is staring at him, trying to see her brother. His hand hangs limp by his side and he looks like a stranger again. She can't comprehend what he has said. It is too much to do all at once. "Wait. How did you get in here? You need a card . . ."

"I walked in after someone."

"We're not supposed to . . . nevermind. What's in Montreal?"

Jeremy lifts his shoulders to his ears. "Dunno. What's in Kingston?"

"I'm in Kingston."

He smiles and the stranger looks like Jeremy again. A taller, leaner version of. And hungry. It occurs to Jo that she should hug him. She holds her arms out and when he sees what she is doing, he does it too. The mechanics are awkward and quick, and somehow they have their arms around each other and she is patting his back. She comes up to his shoulder now and he smells like sweat and stale coffee. The inside of a stranger's pickup. Not bad, all things considered. But this is not how she remembers. And it is not how she imagined.

They have left the door open and Alice walks in as they come apart.

"Hi!" Alice has blond hair. Dreadlocks.

"This is Jeremy," Jo says.

"Hey," Jeremy says. He does not try to shake her hand.

"Hey," Alice says back.

Jo has never had a guy in the room before. She sees how it must look. "Jeremy's family. Is it okay if he stays the night?"

Alice bends one knee and fiddles with the thin strap of a heel behind her back. "A cousin?"

Jo does not look at Jeremy. "Something like that."

They make up a bed on the floor with spare blankets and sleeping bags. Alice hauls the communal vacuum from down the hall to suck up the wood chips.

"I missed you, Joannie," Jeremy says when they are alone.

"It's Jo. I'm Jo now."

Jo is an only child. Jo does not wear glasses. Jo has a fake ID that says she was born in 1977. Jo is not a girl you needed to feel sorry for.

Joan is ten. Jeremy is sixteen. There is a note. Two sentences. *I've gone. Don't try to find me.* The Centre called her parents and her parents called the police. There was a search. The local news media came out. Every night on the TV, her parents crying. *We love you, son. Come home. If anyone has any information . . .*

Patience is a well with a shallow bottom. From up above, it looks deceptive. Go ahead—fall in. You won't drown. People lost interest; they became unkind. Jeremy wasn't kidnapped. He'd gone willingly. What kind of parents were they, anyway? To harbour a drug addict (this was a nice community). To shove him into rehab. To not get him in fast enough. What kind of parents.

Jo wakes up and it is Sunday. Her bed is by the window. A gust of wind rattles the pane. It sounds cold. Victoria Hall is a time warp circa 1968. The carpet is a pukey pink colour like Pepto-Bismol. You must use blue tack on the walls; the posters are always falling down. Sometimes on top of you so that you wake up staring into Liam Howlett's tortured face emerging out of liquid metal.

She hears doors down the hall. Groggy *good mornings.* Slowly the present comes into focus. Jeremy is here. She sits up. A thrill. Christmas morning. In the middle of the room an open space. Bedding in a neat pile. A shard of notebook paper on top. She doesn't want to look. Jo knows what it will say. *I've gone. Don't try to find me.* She closes her eyes. Counts to five. Slowly, slowly. Leans toward the note. On the other side of the room, Alice is a lump under a flowered blanket. Jo stares at the wall, turns her eyes only at the last possible second. What the note says: *Gone to church. Back soon.*

Before Jeremy left, Joan's parents had done things: walked for breast cancer, voted for (more book mobiles) and against (grade five sex-ed) things at PTA meetings, insisted on family dinners. After, they found excuses to skivvy off work. Sometimes on her way to the portables for calculus, she would see them loitering across the street, watching the stoners play with lighters on the edge of the soccer field. (Looking for what? Ghost of teenage son past?) Her brother had left but Joan was the one who disappeared.

"Are you like religious or something?"

They are walking to the library. Alice has gone away for Reading Week. Home to Sudbury. Or Tremblant for skiing. It's not important. She has left her student card behind for

Jeremy to use. Already, they've been to the dining hall in the building with the weird Gaelic name (What was it called? Ban Righ?), where Jo watched Jeremy put away more food than she thought it possible for a human to eat.

"I'm trying it out," Jeremy says. "Sometimes I go to the synagogue too. Depends on what's around."

Jo tallies this up. Give up drugs. Take up God. Grant me the serenity.

Jeremy wears yesterday's shirt—sleeves folded up to the crooks of his elbows (no track marks, she'd surreptitiously checked)—and the same pair of blue jeans. More worn-out than worn-in, the thread at the knees near transparent, threatening to split. As kids, they had called these *potatoes*— the round holes that appeared on the knees of pants or the heels of socks. Mom would say: "Little spuds on my small fries" and Joan and Jeremy would laugh, and inevitably one or the other would demand french fries. It occurs to Jo now, and for the first time, that Jeremy had gone along with the game long after he must have outgrown it.

"So where's the shelter here?" Jo has never seen a homeless shelter. The hands held out from the sidewalk are uniformly young—highschoolers playing at poverty for beer and video-game money.

"The shelter?"

"Well, yeah. If you hadn't seen me, where would you have—"

"Do you want me to leave?" He asks without anger, his voice flat and inscrutable.

"No. God. No. Just curious. Just . . . making conversation."

At first, Jo had been worried that Jeremy looked too dishev-elled, too ratty, that he'd be recognized as an impostor and kicked out of the dining hall. But they had walked in together and Jeremy had slid Alice's student card through the electronic reader and smiled at the woman in the hairnet who watched to make sure bagels didn't get smuggled out. Like this was his morning routine. And Jo saw that her brother had confidence, that he knew how to blend in. Mom and Dad never stood a chance.

"This is kinda like my church," Jo says when they arrive at the library. Stauffer is what a cathedral would look like if it was built in the nineties. From the outside it is fascist, spiky and forbidding. But, through the huge, heavy doors, it soars, full of light. Clean, straight lines. Lots of wood.

Inside, Jeremy drops his cover. He stares up at the vaulting ceiling, the floors of books and reading rooms stacked on top of one another. He is open-mouthed. Jo has to take his hand and force Alice's card through the reader. It is the first time they have touched since the night before. His skin is rough. His wrist bone bobs like an Adam's apple. It is a wrist that belongs to someone else. Granny Edna at the end. She wants to give him a hug. And maybe tuck him into bed, kiss his forehead, and read him a story. *What life have you lived?*

"This place is massive." Jeremy's head is back, crown straining behind neck. "How many square feet?"

"What do I look like, a guide book? I dunno. Big. Let's go upstairs."

She takes him to the undergraduate reading room. They decamp on the best seats in the house: two leather armchairs in front of the fireplace.

Jo gets cracking. The Krebs cycle. Okay.

Jeremy has brought his backpack (it is the same one he ran

away with—a blue beat-up Jansport that looks as though it's shared his life) and his copy of Tolstoy. He'd taken it out the night before.

Tolstoy wrote children's stories?

Yeah. Wanna hear one?

She and Alice had fallen asleep to the sound of her brother's voice, and Jo had dreamed she was six.

Your cousin's cool. Here, take my stud card.

Now, Jeremy is a fidgety reader. After a while, he stands.

"Fireplace reading room," Jo reminds him. "Second floor."

He returns with books. Mill. Augustine. Hume. *Origin of Species. Communist Manifesto. Great Renaissance Painters.* Clamped down under his chin. After that, Jeremy sits still. For hours. Book after book. Covers snapping open, thunking shut. Onion skin turning.

Later, when the window has been black for hours and they finally pack up for the day, Jo says: "Leave the books. Someone will re-file them." Jeremy stacks them neatly in a tower and she watches. Out the corner of her eye. He sees her looking. She turns away.

Ghost of teenager past:

1. Honour Roll
2. Last voice to crack/first face to break out
3. Slayer of imaginary closet monsters
4. Addict, thief, liar

First, their parents had worried about Jeremy having no friends, then they worried about him having the wrong kind of friends. And then he was gone.

Why did he insist on being the odd man out? Always. After a while, he didn't even fit in with the stoners. Pot was a gateway only Jeremy blew through.

A week without classes. What it looks like: Campus quiet. Empty and anxious. Libraries. Common rooms. Dining halls. Writing. Cramming. Muttering. Maslow's hierarchy (physiological/safety/love/esteem/self-actualization). J. Alfred Prufrock (objective dramatic monologue, correlative of melancholy, bathos). Cloud classification (cumulus, stratus, cirrus, nimbus). Atomic number of nitrogen (7). Everyone orbiting around their own nucleus.

Guys wear the same pair of wrinkled jeans day after day. Girls pull back their hair with their hands, not even bothering with brushes, tie it up, and then tuck the ends under, into something that is a cross between a ponytail and a bun. Jo wakes up every morning and puts on an oversized navy blue hoodie. Jeremy wears one of two different-coloured versions of the same shirt. They often walk in a not-uncomfortable silence. Technically, this is grammatically incorrect but it is also true. He is working out different ideas in his head. The things he has read being weighed and assessed. She knows this look.

Joan's university selection criteria:
1. far away
2. far away
3. far away
4. far away

Limestone buildings. Ivy. A guy on a rooftop picking out chords on his guitar. Dress code: cargo pants, GAP sweaters.

Scarves: the more colours, the better. Perfect. She would live in a recruitment poster. She would be girl in V-neck cable-knit on stone step, textbook in lap.

After Jo moved away to school, her parents—suddenly, conveniently—remembered they had a daughter. Inquiries: classes, Alice, weekend plans, prospective boyfriends (Is there anyone special? Be careful. You know condoms are not always . . . Mom! Enough!). And exams! Always exams! As if they were a daily occurrence, as if 99.9 per cent of university wasn't about floating aimlessly with no real conception of how you were faring until after the final. Until after it was too late. Calls, emails; please, God, may no one tell them about ICQ (oh-oh). For the first time, Jo had felt the burden of being an only child.

There is no photo of Joan shaking Principal Harris's hand in a blue gown and stupid hat. Some woman on an online chat room claimed to have seen Jeremy in Seattle.

"Hey, where were you in June? Were you in Seattle?"

"Seattle? No. June, I was in Toronto."

"Are you sure?"

"Yeah. May is pretty foggy but June I know for sure. Toronto."

It is Tuesday and they are walking to the other cafeteria. The one in Leonard Hall. Just for a change. Jeremy wears a thin jean jacket. Jo has given him a scarf and a pair of mitts. She doesn't have anything warmer that would fit. She wears something insubstantial too, an autumn-ish jacket. She wishes he would leave so she could wear her wool coat, but this is a passing thought, one that comes and goes so quickly, it leaves no time for guilt. Jo does not know when Jeremy plans to leave. Or what he is doing here. What she does know: when Alice returns on Sunday, Jeremy will have to go. And: he has been sober since he arrived.

On the first night, she had shoved her vodka to the back of her underwear drawer. Every time she is alone in the room, she takes a ruler to the bottle. Then unscrews the cap and sniffs.

The residence in Leonard Hall is men-only.

"Have you ever been upstairs?" Jeremy asks as they swipe their cards.

"Once. It smelled like Dad's spaghetti."

"What?"

"Dad's . . . the time he put cumin in the pasta?"

Jeremy's face blanks out. An unplugged TV. Someone else's brother. "Nevermind. It smells like a locker room upstairs."

The air in the dining hall is also ripe. Boiled cabbage. Fried liver. Sweet and sour pork. Jo looks around. All week, they have run into people she knows—floormates, lab partners, occasionally a teaching assistant.

Jeremy introduces himself as her cousin. He does it with a straight face and Jo can't tell if he is pissed off or hurt or what. Part of her feels bad but another part of her doesn't want to care.

"The burgers here are good," Jo says. Actually, the food at both dining halls sucks. They should have taken a bus to west campus, where the food is actually half-decent. Tomorrow. Will he still be here? She's afraid to ask. Afraid to spook him. She can't bear to think of him in a shelter.

Jeremy is a ginger, freckles. He does not look like someone who would survive on the streets. And yet, he has.

"What happens next?" Jeremy asks.

They sit across from each other and pick up their forks. Every time they do this, Jo thinks of all the meals she ate facing an empty chair. Her parents at either end of the table. Or more often, absent.

"Next?"

"After this . . . after graduation."

He was her older brother. He was fifteen and she was nine and he knew twelve went into one-forty-four twelve times.

"Something in science, I think." The potatoes are tasteless. She looks for the salt shaker. "But not . . . I don't want to be a doctor."

"What's your major?"

"Bio for now but we'll see. I might switch to biochemistry."

"Biochemistry." He repeats the word and she tries to remember if biochemistry was part of her vocabulary at age sixteen.

She complains about her lab partner instead. "She doesn't trust me. We split up the work and then she does my half before I can even get started."

"Sounds like a pretty good set-up." Jokey.

"She doesn't even give me a chance! She wants to be a nurse."

Jo could just see her butting in during surgery, snatching the scalpel from the surgeon's gloved hand.

"Nurses are bitches."

Jo smiles. It takes her a moment to see he is not joking.

They walk along the lakefront. Jo shows Jeremy the outdoor sculpture—two rectangles rising out of the ground, tilted and leaning toward each other—and explains how they were built on a fault line.

"They're supposed to touch at the turn of the century."

Jeremy looks up. From some angles, from farther away, the two columns can look like they already connect. Lovers in mid-embrace. But from here, from close range, what is most evident is the gap. A peaked roof with a hole in the middle. An imperfect shelter.

"I think they miscalculated," he says.

He takes the incline at a run. Jo wants to yell for him to be careful. For a moment he's at the summit—right shoe on the edge of one rectangle, left shoe on the other. Poised. Suspended at the top, between two mountains. Behind, trees. Naked branches. His head becomes a moon eclipsing the sun. Backlit, his body is a shadow. Jo's hand forms a visor. She squints. Then he runs down the other side. Fast.

When he is most like Jeremy: first thing in the mornings, last thing at night. Reading aloud from Tolstoy. The steady cadence of his voice, a sleigh drawn by horses through a snowy Russian landscape.

When she watches him with others—librarians, people on her floor, and later, at the bus station ticket counter—then, he is a stranger.

Sometimes Jeremy takes off. Needs air. To be alone. Never very long. An hour. And a half, tops. On Thursday Jo puts on her wool coat. Pulls up the hood. Keeps her distance. He walks with his head down. Man on a mission. Years since she's watched him walk. All week she has only seen it side-on. Now she sees the place where the rubber soles of his shoes peel away. The stick-thinness of his legs. The hunch of his shoulders.

Earlier that day, she had come into the room with an empty laundry basket to find him standing by her desk, holding a photo of Mom and Dad.

"How are they?"

"Broken." The word had left her mouth. It could not be taken back.

Jeremy slumped into himself. He put down the picture frame.

"I screwed up, Joannie."

"It's not too late. Why don't you—"

"No. I can't."

"You came here."

"I didn't plan that. It just happened."

Jo is a magnet. Jeremy was drawn. Against his will.

"They're better off without me," he had said.

Did he think that was noble? It was selfish. No one was better off.

University Avenue past the library. Three students come out. At the corner, a handful more. An impromptu crowd and for a step or two she loses track of which one is Jeremy. Another cold day. Jeremy's hands fist up. She knows without seeing. Halfway down Johnson Street: church bells. Jeremy walks a little faster. Jo stops. Up ahead is St. Mary's. People on the steps. Walking in. Grounding out butt ends. They look like Jeremy. And they don't. After that, there is no need to check for track marks.

Heroin is different. Is what Jeremy says. It's like nothing else. "When the smack was in me, I had no problems."

The problems of middle-class two-parent suburbia. Jo tries to think what these could be.

All the bad things, being high is the opposite. Anxiety, inadequacy, they're clustered up here. At the cold North Pole. And way over there, Antarctica, is being high. Nothing could be wrong in the world when Jeremy was high. *He* could do no wrong.

"It was like everything before was darkness and being high was the light."

And now? Was life black?

More like grey. "I'm learning to live with grey."

Jo still doesn't know what any of this has to do with Mom and Dad and why he won't call them. She has patiently waited. Since the first night. Now, it is Friday and time is running out.

Simultaneous: "What's with this tree stump?"/"Call them. They won't be mad or whatever."

Jeremy shakes his head, stares at the poster that hangs like a headboard over her bed.

On their walks through campus, Jo has only shown Jeremy the nicest parts. She wishes he had come in September, when everything looked scholastic and preppy instead of dismal and plaid. She has been hawking an idea, a subtle suggestion. She does not think he is buying.

Jo gives up. "Alice whittles."

"Whittles?" The beginnings of a grin.

"With a pen knife. Swiss Army." Jo flicks a shaving of bark with her toe. "The shape has yet to reveal itself."

Laughter. Relief.

Sometimes they speak of the past. Before the drugs. Always before. The time he taught her to ride a bike. Holding the handlebar and seat. Then just the seat, by the very edge. Until she lost track of the moment he was holding on and the next when she rode free. A split second that moved from present into past unacknowledged.

When Jeremy ran away, out of her present and into her past. When? The exact time un-noted. How long before anyone realized? Her parents in meetings. Markers on flip charts. Until someone knocked on the door. *Excuse me. Urgent phone call.* Joan at the chalkboard. Conjugating irregular verbs. Until the vice principal walked in. *Bring your books with you.* A classroom of eyes on her back. Then and after. Always after. And now here is Jeremy. Catapulted out of her past and into her present. Three-dimensional. A guy who both is and isn't her brother.

Her whole life. Every moment ever after. An exercise in re-creation. Taking up the pieces, working out how they fit. Liquor bottles topped up with water. The sharp chemical smell like concentrated detergent that made her head spin. The piggy bank. Smashed. Slamming doors. Red eyes. Long-sleeved shirts in summer. Report cards. Calls from the principal. Things she witnessed but only later understood.

Jeremy's old room is there still. A museum no one visits. She wants to tell him but holds back, waiting. A reckoning. On one side, her hurt. On the other, his. Make the two sides equal.

There is a schedule. Little boxes shaded in different colours. Taped, it hangs down from the shelf that juts out over Jo's desk. She does not worry about midterms. She works hard. Of course, there is hard work. But there is also a formula. Scantron. Due dates. These are things over which she has control.

Evenings are for revision. Jo and Jeremy sit in her room and he reads quietly or drills her. A tape is in the machine. Volume on low. Portishead on one side. Tricky on the other. The music is languid and lazy. Like floating underwater. Like drowning. Like dying.

In Jo's textbook there are diagrams of viruses. Each one is a funeral wreath made of different kinds of flowers. She closes the book, stares at the ceiling above her bed, and tries to recall the genomic structure of HIV. A retrovirus. Genus lentivirus. Measured in nanometres. The size of a speck.

"Why not medicine?" Jeremy asks.

"Too much school," Jo says. Two strands of RNA at the centre. Protein shell like a pearl necklace. "Too much expensive school."

"Dr. Joannie Halsham. I like the sound of that."

Average latency: ten years. A squatter taking up residence, settling in for the long haul. HIV is small and cunning. It knows how to hide.

"There are easier ways to be a doctor."

Jo has thought about graduate school. But not in any serious way. She is eighteen and time is still a luxury.

Jeremy sits on Alice's bed. Cross-legged, bodhisattva-like. Jo's psychology text is in his lap. He has quizzed her on Piaget (*Four stages of childhood development. Go!*), but now she's moved on to biology.

Sometimes, Jo can fool herself into thinking. Sometimes, she can look at Jeremy and think: If my brother had never been an addict, this is how he would be.

"You'd be a great doctor." Jeremy scratches his chin and turns a page. "You have the people smarts. Bedside manner."

"Yeah, you're the expert, right?" The words that tumble out

are those of a younger sister teasing an older brother. Normal people. But after she has spoken and it cannot be taken back and Jeremy has not lobbed back a joke of his own, she remembers. That she does not know. Anything about him.

Jeremy leaves on Sunday. Overnight it snows but only very lightly, and in the morning the temperature spikes and everything is dripping and melty. At the bus station, Jeremy skirts the puddles without looking. Jo is glad about the twenties. An envelope shoved to the bottom of his bag. No time for a letter and anyway, what would she write?

The bus hasn't arrived yet and they stand awkwardly by the folding plastic chairs. One week ago he had gone to church and left her a note. This. This is the moment when present becomes past.

Alice is due back in the afternoon. Jeremy used her card for the last time at breakfast, and afterwards, they'd snuck out bagels and fruit and a couple pieces of cutlery for the road. Jo told him about how when it snowed students would steal trays and use them to go sliding down the hill beside the dining hall. At the exit, Jeremy and the woman in the hairnet had exchanged good mornings. Old friends now.

"I'll be here in the summer," Jo says now at the bus station. "I got a job. There's an ice cream parlour downtown . . ."

Already there's a fantasy—she's scooping rocky road, hand cramped up, and her brother saunters in, cool as you like. Jo feels furious. Angry at herself for indulging in this daydream and angry at him because he will not come.

"It's nice here," Jeremy says. "I'm glad you're a part of it." He nods his head and glances around, as if they are standing on the green in front of Theological Hall instead of the sticky floor at the bus station. He reminds Jo of their father, of something he would say and the exact way he would say it. Her anger turns a little to the left and then it is regret.

She wants to pummel and shake him. *Take a class. Why not? Don't leave.*

He does not say: Sorry for interrupting your cramming, or, Thanks for putting me up. There are unsaid things between them but also no platitudes.

I'm glad we had this week, is what he says. "Now when I think of you, it'll be in context."

The bus is announced at the same moment it pulls up. Around them, people stand and heave up bags. It is not quite nine and the other passengers go through these motions with exaggerated exhaustion, as if they are Herculean efforts.

"You know where to find me. For the next three and a half years anyway." Jo will not see him again. Already, she knows this. "Just. Send a postcard or something."

They go outside. Jeremy has his ticket in his hand. It is white and perforated. This time the hug is just right. The way she remembers. The way she imagines. Jo holds her brother close and inhales the scent of her own soap, her Pears shampoo. He is thin and insubstantial. In Montreal, he will disappear. A speck in the crowd.

"Wait," she calls as he turns to leave. She peels off her sweatshirt and holds it out to him. She hasn't got a jacket and now the February air bites her bare arms. "It's cold in Montreal."

Jeremy holds it close for a second, hands crossed, knuckles turned in. Then he shrugs off his jean jacket and pulls it on over his head. The university's name is splashed across the front. The tail of the *Q* trails out like a ribbon. The sweatshirt has always been big on Jo, but on Jeremy, it is a perfect fit.

She does not ask why he is going to Montreal. Why not somewhere warmer. Instead she touches the lines around his eyes. "You need to wear sunscreen."

"It's February."

"At least SPF 15."

"Bye, sis."

He's trying to keep things light, to be silly. But Jo's feelings have seized her and now she wants to seize him too. *Don't go. Not yet.*

Everyone is on the bus. The luggage compartment underneath has closed and the driver is waiting.

Jeremy hands over his ticket for inspection. He is about to put a foot on the stair.

Jo grabs his arm. "You need to take the medication." She speaks quietly. Looks him steady in the eyes. Her heart beats hard. She did not know she would say this and now the words have taken them both by surprise. "Don't miss a dose. Not a single one. It's really important."

"I won't," Jeremy says. "I promise. I swear, Joannie. I promise."

She can't recall what she said next. If there was anything. If it was just a nod or a smile or a look or maybe another hug. She can only remember her heart like a fist jamming up her throat. He waved from the window and then the bus rolled away and then that was it.

Years later, when the memory of this week has grown so vague she must reconstruct the details, an old photograph will remind Jo that Jeremy was at camp the summer her training wheels came off. It was her dad who taught her how to ride a bike.

JACK WANG

THE NATURE OF THINGS

As the train pulled out of Shanghai South Station, Alice buried her face in her hands. The train had been late, and she and Frank had waited for over two hours, the platform swelling, restless. When the train finally arrived, they found themselves caught in the onrush of those scrambling for third class. At first Frank had kept an arm around her, pushing as they went, but when a boy being dragged by his mother lost his grip and fell, Frank let go. When she looked back, he was roping off the crowd with outstretched arms to keep the boy from being trampled. "Don't stop, Alice! Get on the train!" Those were his parting words.

Two days earlier, on what became known as Black Saturday, Frank had been called to the hospital. According to both English and Chinese reports, the Great World bombing had been an accident. After being clipped by Japanese warships on the river, a Chinese pilot had tried to lighten his load on the grounds of the Shanghai Racecourse, only to fall hundreds of yards short. Incredibly, Chinese bombs had also fallen on the

Bund, right on the corner of Nanking Road. All told, nearly two thousand dead, more injured. Alice had tethered herself to the radio, waiting for Frank to come home.

"You need to stay with my aunt and uncle," he said when he returned.

She would have gladly taken the next train to Wuhu, two hundred miles to the west, as he was urging, but she noticed the pronoun he used. "*I* should stay with them?"

"I can't leave. Not now."

"Frank, this is war."

"Exactly."

For weeks, she had heard the insouciance of Shanghailanders in public, the British especially, who discussed impending war as if betting on horses, or worse, aggrieved by the prospect of rain on a picnic. So she loved Frank, she really did, for caring. Nonetheless, she felt a flare of resentment. They had come to Shanghai for his sake. Everything they had ever done was for him. She wanted him to put her first for once.

"We have to think about the baby."

"Which is why you should go."

"I don't want to have this baby without you."

She only meant that she wanted him to deliver their child, but they both heard the implications.

"I'll be fine. Both sides respect the Concession. This is practically France."

"Then I'm staying too."

Even as she said this, she felt the dark impulse. Yes, she was professing love, resolve, fear of separation, but she was also trying to saddle his conscience: if you stay, you'll endanger all three of us.

But he wouldn't give in. As always, his mind was made up. They argued to exhaustion, until she relented. If she couldn't save Frank, she had to save herself. And their child.

Frank and Alice had known each other all their lives, ever since they were urchins scrabbling over the one and only playground in Vancouver's Chinatown. They both went to Strathcona Elementary, then King Edward High School, where Frank had been something of a wonder boy. Once, using only household materials—screws, wire, tin foil, Mason jars—and a neon sign transformer, he built his own little Tesla coil and held her hand to it, closer and closer until a purple spark leapt from the ring to the tip of her finger. No one was surprised that he wanted to go to medical school, even though he couldn't be a doctor, not really, at least not in Canada. To join the Royal College of Physicians— or any professional society, for that matter—you had to be registered to vote, but in 1930 the Chinese didn't have the vote.

"I don't want to move to America," she protested softly once, reluctant to leave her mother, her father, her three younger siblings.

"Don't worry, I'll find a way."

That was Frank for you, so certain he was special, that he alone would beat the odds. With no medical school in town, though, he had to go to Toronto. Whenever he was gone, she felt doubly aware of life, first as she lived through it, then through her missives to Frank. Every spring when he returned, her letters came back in their own leather duffle, like salmon home to spawn. But after six long, lonely years, when he finally came back for good, he couldn't find a job. Nothing had changed. No one would hire him.

At the end of that summer, as Alice worked on the seating plan for their reception, Frank announced that he had found work. Apparently some classmates, ashamed, had begged around, and someone knew someone who knew someone at Hôpital Sainte-Marie.

"Where's that?"

"Shanghai."

"Oh, Frank," she said, eyes dampening.

Their honeymoon began with a voyage aboard the *Empress of Japan*. As a gift, Frank's father, a merchant, sent them first class. By day, they walked the decks, lost themselves in reading rooms, swam in the indoor pool; by night, they dined on turtle consommé and roasted leg of lamb and danced to "Goody Goody" and "A Fine Romance." At the end of ten days, after stops in Honolulu, Yokohama, and Kobe, they reached teeming, sprawling, magnificent Shanghai. They stayed at the Palace Hotel, right on the Bund, which might have been Europe if not for the rickshaws and sampans. Still on honeymoon, they played tourist at places like Yuyuan Bazaar, where the little steamer buns were the best they'd ever had, and for one heady week she was glad they had come.

Then they moved to a terraced house in the French Concession, and Frank started his rounds. He put in long hours, longer than he had to, from love of work and a need to prove himself. Shanghai was a veritable army of foreign doctors, and he was foreign-but-not-foreign. On the days she waited for him to come home, for life to resume in his presence, she felt a reprise of their time apart, all those abject years of waiting in Vancouver. She made a point to venture out, only to encounter the city's underside. Once, on Avenue Joffre, she saw a woman curse a rickshaw driver in French, then slap him across the face with a set of wrist-length gloves. Another time, she came to a little park whose first rule, posted on a sign outside, was *The Gardens are reserved for the Foreign Community*. All of this made Shanghai feel painfully familiar.

After a long bleak winter, she started getting sick in the mornings. Then in July, trouble came down from the north. One night, a Japanese company stationed near Peking set off on night manoeuvres. When one of the soldiers failed to return, they traded shots with the Chinese around the Marco Polo Bridge. It turned out the missing soldier had gone to visit a brothel, but it hardly mattered now; the wheels of war had been greased. Back in 1931, after the Mukden Incident, Generalissimo Chiang had conceded Manchuria. It was too far away, and his army simply wasn't ready. Six years later, his dream of sixty well-trained and well-equipped divisions was still just that, a dream, even with help from the Germans, friendly for the moment, but all talk now was of taking on the "dwarf bandits." Frank assured Alice that any fighting would be far from Shanghai. Still, when the Japanese took Peking before the month was out, she was alarmed—and for good reason, it turned out. The open country of the north would have made cannon fodder of the Chinese Army. The Generalissimo had saved his troops for the only place they had a fighting chance: the alleyways of Shanghai.

———

Frank's uncle and aunt—*her* uncle and aunt, as she thought of them now—were all doting chatter, a blizzard of Mandarin, when they met her at the station in Wuhu. She had only met them once before in Shanghai, yet her uncle waved on tiptoe, glasses glinting, and her aunt looped an arm through hers as if they were sisters. In the car—a chauffeured Lincoln Zephyr, sleek as a beetle—they sat one to each side in the back seat and plied her with food, steamed bread as white as snow and hard-boiled eggs crazed with black tea and soy.

The Yeungs dealt in Chinese medicine. This explained the family fortune, a brother at either end of a trans-Pacific enterprise. Though Alice wanted nothing more than to be alone, she didn't protest when her in-laws took her to an apothecary filled with desiccated jars and dark ring-pulled drawers and showed her off to their employees.

It wasn't until bedtime that Alice was finally left to unpack. At the bottom of her suitcase, she found a clothbound book she didn't recognize, a stowaway. She turned to the title page:

LUCRETIUS

ON THE NATURE OF THINGS

(*DE RERUM NATURA*)

TRANSLATED

BY

T.E. WALLACE

M.A., FELLOW OF TRINITY COLLEGE, CAMBRIDGE

She shouldn't have been surprised. Before they were married at First United, they had argued over a church wedding.

For her parents, church was a salve for toiling ignobly in a distant country, her father for so many years in a cannery that his cutting hand was now a frozen claw. For Frank, though, church was just a way of aping respectability. He was no heathen; he didn't need to be saved. He was always looking for his own way and seemed to find it in a bookstore in the International Settlement. More than once in the past year, he had tried to describe *De rerum natura* with a wild-eyed air of discovery. Alice herself was a woman of no great piety. If she used to go to church in Vancouver, it was largely for her parents' sakes. Even so, she couldn't abide the things Frank said. What did he mean there was no God? God was as plain to her as her very existence. Irritated anew, she put the book back and shut her suitcase. Out of habit, she got to her knees and prayed.

The next day she received the first of his telegrams. That was the deal, a telegram every day. To save on coding, his telegrams were short, sometimes just a single Chinese character: home. That was enough to let her breathe again.

At the end of the week, she walked to a nearby hotel, closeted herself in a booth, slipped in a bronze token, and sat under slatted light for a few timed minutes.

"How are you feeling?" he asked.

Despite the bitter concoctions her in-laws insisted she drink, she felt rundown—and thirsty, always thirsty—but she didn't want to rouse the doctor in him. "Fine."

"Got our first from the frontlines."

She knew from XGOA, the government radio station in

Nanking, that the Chinese had launched a massive assault on the Japanese Marine Headquarters in Hongkew. "And?"

From the silence, she could tell it had been worse than he'd imagined.

"I thought the nurses were brave."

Not for the first time, she wondered if he didn't feel something for one of the nurses. Under the wingspan of their wimples, the sisters could be startlingly beautiful. She had hoped her absence would tug at him, bring him to her sooner rather than later, but now she sensed some still greater devotion being forged in the crucible of the operating room.

If she were still in Shanghai, they would have been strolling arm in arm to Avenue Joffre for *zakuski*, little plates of smoked salmon, salted herring, pickled tomatoes, and the like, which went down well with warming shots of vodka, especially in winter. She could have said something affectionate like, "I miss Tkachenko." Instead she complained that Wuhu was provincial: no Little Moscow here. Before she could finish, a woman came on to tell them their time was up. Now was the moment to soften, to say something effusive, but all she managed was "Bye, dear. Talk to you next week."

At first there were hopes the war would be short. The goal was to drive the enemy out in one fell swoop. In the Japanese stronghold of Yangtzepoo downtown, where crossroads were staunchly defended by sandbag trenches, gun nests, and brambles of barbed wire, the Chinese managed despite a lack of cover to claw all the way down to Broadway, the last street before the river, but were finally stopped by the high walls of the wharf. The Japanese, nearly driven into the sea, held out long enough for reinforcements to arrive.

No, the war would not be short.

Incensed that China was putting up a fight, the Japanese bombed the city. Air-raid sirens became a daily, sometimes hourly occurrence. If Alice could sleep at night, it was only because she knew the French Concession went largely unscathed; only the Chinese districts lay in smouldering ruin. Still, she kept urging Frank to leave.

"Might be safer now to stay put."

He had a point. Even the South Station had been bombed, much to her disbelief. Women and children mostly, trying to flee as she had. But the soundness of his logic only made her angry. What he should have wanted above all else was to come to her. To them.

Once, a fellow doctor had tried to take Frank to the Shanghai Club, famed for its forty-foot-long bar where patrons sat in order of rank, taipans at the end with the best view of the Bund, but nowhere along its length was there a place for someone like him. "He's a doctor! He's Canadian!" his colleague had argued, to no avail; Frank was turned away and came home burning. His staying behind in Shanghai had something to do with being Chinese, which almost made her sympathetic. But it seemed like foolish pride to stick it out at any cost.

A month passed and her belly grew. She found herself capsized in bed, crabwalking in and out of chairs. The fitful limbs that stretched her belly made her think of an insect trapped in spider's silk, so she started calling the baby "Bug." She tried

to entice Frank to leave with details of what he was missing—
"You need to see this. It's really amazing"—and those were
the moments when he seemed closest to coming.

Alice was surprised that in her state her body keened for
Frank's. Every summer when he came back from Toronto,
they would frequent the pool at Kitsilano Beach—the largest
saltwater pool in the world. They weren't barred from entering, but they got their share of looks. Frank always insisted on
going. Not only that, he would make a point to swim the
pool's length, all two hundred yards, in just a few breaths, then
rise from the pool like Johnny Weissmuller himself, slicking
his hair in both hands. Sometimes, after stealing kisses all day,
he would whisper, "I can't wait anymore," but despite being
drunk from too much sun and feeling him through his wool-
len bathing shorts, she always insisted on waiting. Now those
summers seemed like lost time.

September dragged into October. With each passing week,
Frank seemed to grow more morose. Their weekly phone
conversations were blighted by ever longer stretches of silence,
precious, expensive seconds they couldn't afford to fritter
away. "What's the matter, Frank?" she would ask, trying to
bring him back, but she knew: the carnage was taking its toll.
She asked Frank's uncle to speak to his brother and wrote her
parents asking the same. If Frank wouldn't leave as a husband
and father, maybe he would leave as a son.

In early November, an unexpected landing at Hangchow Bay,
twenty miles from Shanghai. For weeks, the Japanese had been
pushing down from the north from the Yangtze River; now they

were also coming from the south. The objective was clear: outflank the city. The pincer was poised. Frank had to get out.

"Sister Marguerite thinks I should leave."

"Don't *you* think you should leave?"

Only the slightest pause before he said, "Yes, it's time," wearily.

Alice soared. "Thank God."

For some reason the line went cold. Strange that he should seem low at the prospect of reunion. "What's the matter, darling? You seem blue."

At first he couldn't say. Then in a faltering voice: "I wanted to win. I wanted to beat the damn Japs."

Alice discovered newfound energy for her daily circuit around Mirror Lake, over the bridges and under the willows for a good half mile. "Daddy's coming, Bug, Daddy's coming," she would coo, cradling her belly. She wished Frank were only a train ride away, but rail was still too dangerous, so his plan was to catch a ride to Taihu Lake and cross by boat, then hitch a ride or walk the rest of the way. From the west side of the lake, Wuhu was only a hundred miles.

Only three days after Frank set off, Shanghai fell, more quickly than expected, but Alice felt triumphant: he had made it out in time. All that was left was to conquer whatever distance remained. Every day she did the math, the number of miles he must have been travelling. The hardest part was no longer receiving telegrams. After a steady diet, it was painful to go without, but Frank had warned her not to expect them.

Four, five, six days passed. Each one brought rising hopes in the morning, creeping doubts at night. After a week she gave in to dread and called the hospital. With the indubitability of a head nurse, Sister Marguerite said she had last seen Frank five days ago. In fact, it was in the log.

"Was there an emergency?" Alice asked.

"My dear," Sister Marguerite replied, "it's all an emergency."

Two days. Frank had stayed two more days without telling her. At first in her confusion she felt relieved. The hands of time whirled back a full forty-eight hours, making it more likely that he was still en route. Then darker thoughts invaded. What could possibly have kept him and why didn't he say? Suddenly her husband seemed someone wholly unknown to her. More painful still was the possibility, now distinct, that he'd been caught up in the chaotic Chinese retreat. With the enemy in pursuit, the troops had broken rank. At Taihu Lake, it was every man for himself. In the struggle for passage, young and old alike got pushed under. She had thought Frank had escaped all that. Now all she could picture was him stupidly saving others before saving himself.

Every day from dawn till dusk, she sat outside, scanning the street, waiting for the first glimpse, the ecstatic moment, but it never came. Another week passed without any sign. By this point the Japanese had started marching toward Nanking. She had thought that the war would end with the fall of Shanghai, but the Japanese were not only pressing on but taking their pound of flesh. Throughout the countryside, villages were being torched. When she heard that men were being bound in groups, doused with gasoline, and set ablaze, she had to steady herself. In hindsight, it was obvious that Frank should have stayed put. After the city fell, thousands stretched their arms through the iron fence of the French Concession, so many they had to be held off with tanks. Everyone desperate to get in, and she had made him get out. In the small hours of night, Alice would curse herself, then Frank, then curse herself for cursing him. At unbidden moments, she fell to her knees, bartered with God. Sometimes she prayed it was all an elaborate ruse. That a letter would soon explain how he had taken a ship to France with one of the sisters, now defrocked. Anything to know he was still alive.

The Army kept falling back. The so-called "Chinese Hindenburg Line" was supposed to hold out for six months; it fell in two weeks. The Generalissimo took to the airwaves to announce that the government was moving to Chungking. That's when her uncle released his employees. The Japanese were not only closing in on Nanking but also making a break for Wuhu to cut off any retreat. Everyone had to leave.

"We have a family compound upriver," her uncle explained.

"What about Frank?" Alice blurted.

He touched a pensive hand to his glasses. "You two go first. I'll wait another day."

Her aunt made as if to speak but checked herself. It wasn't for her to object; it was for Alice to decline. But she couldn't bring herself to pull up the lifeline, to feign refusal.

When she went to pack, she found it again, the book Frank had given her, rearing up like an apparition. She ran a hand down its grainy cloth cover and pressed her nose to the open pages, inhaling the scent of paper and glue. Then she filled her suitcase and laid the book on top.

At dusk they made their way down to the Clearwater River, less a river than a turbid, slow-moving stream. At the sight of the rickety-looking skiff, Alice wavered, afraid it would tip under her weight. But with help from her aunt aboard and her uncle ashore, she managed to sidle in. The skiff swayed, then steadied.

"See you soon!" her uncle cried, too brightly.

A young ferryman punted them upriver. For a while the only sounds were the drip and plash of his pole, but after darkness fell the sounds were obscured by a drone. At first it sounded like bees in a glade; then it took on a whirring mechanical edge. Sure enough, a constellation of black stars slid fiendishly across the sky. Then came whistling, flashes, thunderous claps. Downriver, fireballs ripped through the dark. Alice looked away, stricken by guilt, but her aunt was resolute: "He'll be fine. He knows what to do."

At first light, her aunt pounded on the gate of the family compound. *"Lao Ch'ang! K'uai tien k'ai men!"* she shouted. Moments later, a wizened man appeared at the door and lead them through the inner gate. The compound was a quadrangle with mulberry trees in the courtyard. After a sleepless night, Alice collapsed in one of the side rooms.

In the afternoon, she went back down to the river to look for her uncle. She brought Frank's book as a kind of talisman, but when the day stalled, she started leafing through. The book began with an invocation of Venus: "Mother of Rome, delight of Gods and men . . . " When the first stanzas proved elusive, she riffled ahead until she saw a passage underlined in pencil:

. . . for behold whenever
The sun's light and the rays, let in, pour down
Across dark halls of houses: thou wilt see
The many mites in many a manner mixed
Amid a void in the very light of the rays,
And battling on, as in eternal strife,
And in battalions contending without halt,
In meetings, partings, harried up and down.

The commonplace of dust. What did this mean and why did Frank care? He never mentioned giving her the book, never asked if she read it, but now his markings seemed to speak, to hold the key to why he had stayed. Her last glimpse of Frank had not been of him hovering over the boy and holding back the crowd at the South Station. Instead, it came after the platform had thinned, as the train began to creak, when Frank ran up to her car and leapt to kiss her window, which startled her and made her snort. All the way to Wuhu, she had studied the smear of his lips, wishing she could reach through the glass and somehow preserve that scintilla of him. That's how she felt now, studying his markings, that Frank was near yet unreachable.

Intermittent traffic on the river. Sampans laden with bundles, children, chicken coops. But no sign of anyone she knew.

In the morning she awoke to commotion in the courtyard. From her bed she heard a man's voice—her uncle's—describing how he had cowered all night, waiting for the bombs to stop. He would have gotten here sooner if not for the Army commandeering everything.

As soon as she opened her door, he said, "I left word with the neighbours. Frank will know where to go."

She had hoped Frank would be here too. Still, she was buoyed by the sight of her uncle.

"He's coming. I feel it," she said.

Far from dashing her hopes, her uncle bolstered them: on his trip upriver, he heard that a Chinese general had disguised himself as a peasant in order to evade the Japanese. Maybe Frank had done something like that, she thought. Or maybe he had sprained his knee or twisted an ankle and knew better than to push it. Maybe he was holed up somewhere, nursing himself, biding his time. Anything was possible.

All day, she sat on the banks of the river, half-hidden in saw-grass. Again, she brought Frank's book, and when time dragged she studied his markings. Many converged around the idea that the universe was made of atoms—indivisible, indestructible. That much she could accept. But no sooner did she start to nod along than she found herself unsettled. "So from the body if mind and spirit be withdrawn, / Total collapse of all must follow . . . " The passage went on in that vein, and despite the prettified language, she sensed its meaning, and it troubled her, she who had grown up not only in the Church but in Chinatown, with all its talk of ghosts. One morning aboard the *Empress of Japan*, Alice had run into two "grandfathers" from Chinatown. Both were pressing shabby hats to their heads, afraid they would blow away, and one had a face so mottled with age it might have been splattered with ink. Both were travelling steerage but had somehow managed to find her. *"Kung-hsi! Kung-hsi!"* they cried, pleased that the "little dumpling" of Chinatown had finally gotten married. Now here were men who knew the ravages of time and distance, who had only seen their wives a few times in decades, on those rare occasions when they went back to China. Men for whom a mere six years would have been a mercy. Most of these men were now too poor or too ashamed of their poverty to move back to China, but the Great Depression came bearing an unexpected gift: a ticket home in exchange for the promise never to come back, which was cheaper for the powers that be than offering relief. And this made the old men happy. They were going home to die. Their ghosts wouldn't be doomed to wander Gold Mountain forever.

What was Frank trying to say through the book? That these men were wrong? That it didn't matter where they died? It bothered her, his skepticism, and the feeling that he was trying to disabuse her of something.

She set the book down and gazed at the river, where traffic today was heavier. What she saw mostly were ragged bands of soldiers, rifles in hand, cigarettes dangling. At one point, a young, hungry-looking soldier spied her on the banks—alone, supine, bursting with life—and kept his eyes fixed as his skiff puddled past. He stared with such intent that she was sure he would leap off the skiff and splash toward her, drenching himself as he went. By the time he cleared the bend, her heart was surging painfully. Not just from fear but also the knowledge that she hadn't looked away.

In her guilt, she recalled something Frank had told her, that despite once being widely read, *De rerum natura* virtually disappeared during the Middle Ages until a rare medieval copy was found in a monastery during the Renaissance. That, she decided, was what Frank was really trying to say, that he too would slip through the bottleneck. That he and he alone would come to her.

It took a day for Alice to realize they should have been on the move too, that her in-laws were tarrying for her sake, letting her keep vigil. "If we have to leave . . . " she said in the morning, and her in-laws nodded, relieved.

As her uncle gathered food, she helped her aunt sew money into the lining of their clothes. Before they could finish, however, the family servant, Old Chang, burst through the inner gate and locked it frantically behind him. "*Jih-pen-ren lai-le!*" he gasped. "Are you sure?" her uncle asked. The old man nodded. "White bandanas," he said, tying an imaginary one to his head. "On the crest of the hill." Her uncle's brow buckled. He looked at Alice, at her distension, and said, "It's too late to run. We have to hide."

"Where?" his wife asked.

Her uncle surveyed the house in his mind, then strode to the very back, to a long, narrow, dimly lit room with a marble counter along its length, atop which sat two candles, a platter of oranges, a censer full of charred stalks, and dozens of red and gold funeral plaques, rising like buildings in a model city. The altar room.

Below the counter was a cabinet with a small door. Her uncle slid it open.

Her aunt peered. "Are you sure?"

"We have no choice."

Her aunt lowered herself to the floor. Out of modesty, she sat down and backed in, so it seemed she was not so much entering as being swallowed whole. "Are you all right?" her uncle asked once she was in. "Yes, yes," she replied impatiently, her voice already cavernous. Alice sat down, helped by her uncle and Old Chang, the stone floor plungingly cold. After walking her haunches over the lip of the door, she slid back, hands pocked with grit. She should have loosed her bun, which would have given her poor neck an extra inch of space. As it was, she sat with her face nearly pressed to the sudden monstrosity of her belly.

"After I get in," her uncle instructed Old Chang, "put some stools in front of the altar. Then unlock the gates. If they can't get in, they'll burn the house down. Open some drawers, make it look like we've left in a hurry. Then climb onto the roof and stay out of sight. Don't come down till they're gone. Can you manage that?" Alice heard no reply, only what sounded like a clap on the back, and she pictured a lifetime of fealty, Old Chang carrying a boy on his shoulders. Then her uncle got in and the world went dark.

The slap and shuffle of Old Chang's slippers, retreating, returning, retreating again. Stools scraped, drawers whinnied, and then the house fell silent. Alice would have felt safer in total darkness, her body dematerialized, but a gap between two panels let in a spray of light, enough to prove that she was still there. If she angled her head just so, she could see out, the breach sharpening the room like a lens, and this made her fear the opposite, that someone might see in, catch her eyes glinting in darkness. So she closed them and in that more complete darkness wondered how her life had come to this.

If her ghost were left to wander here, would it feel lost or at home?

A pounding at the gate. Belligerent shouts, muffled, remote, then ringingly clear. Footsteps in the house, dozens of sets, it seemed, all scurrying toward them. The splintering of wood, the bursting tinkle of china, and raucous laughter, all strangely amplified by the roaring in her ears.

In no time, footsteps were outside the altar-room door, where they slowed, quieted. With what seemed like caution, unseen figures entered. Had they heard something? Was one already holding a finger to his lips and pointing? Out of sheer terror, Alice opened her eyes. Through the breach, she glimpsed camel-toed shoes, tightly wrapped puttees, and the dull gleam of a bayonet.

She prayed, hard.

As if in answer, the soldiers muttered and left. Alice couldn't tell how long she was forced to stay there, tensed in silence, waiting for the soldiers to finish ransacking the house, but by the time Old Chang came padding back, every muscle in her body yowled for release. There was no more blood in her legs. She could hardly stand. But she was alive.

"They were afraid," her uncle said. "They have no mercy for the living, but they still respect the dead."

If not God, then ghosts. Someone had saved them.

Suddenly Alice was in flight. She ran to her room and tore through the clothes that now lined the floor. And there it still was, her book.

"We can't stay," Old Chang said. "More are coming to spend the night. I heard them."

Warm beds. Provisions. Of course they would be back. But the four of them couldn't exactly run, not with the enemy everywhere. Better to let the first wave pass and take their chances later.

In a copse beyond the house was a wooden shed, her uncle said. They could spend the night there. As soon as they gathered themselves, they dared the few hundred yards to the woods, the men lugging a ladder between them. When they came to the battered shed and its makeshift boards, Old Chang clambered onto the roof and Alice was made to follow. The ladder was then raised and thrust down through the skylight, and she climbed down. Only then did she understand the elaborate entrance: the shed was full of rice. She stifled laughter, sinking into the unexpected dune.

The ladder retracted and reappeared until all of them were safely in. There on the rice, they made little beds for themselves, Alice relieved for something reasonably solid against the small of her back. Within the hour, the coughing of engines, followed by drunken revelry long into the night.

Sometime in the night, Alice awoke from a dream she instantly forgot. The others were still asleep, her in-laws huddled for warmth, Old Chang off in a corner, and the shed unexpectedly bright. The gloaming that had fizzled in like a mist was now a clear shaft of moonlight, teeming, undulant, alive. Motes of dust they must have kicked up themselves were still floating, spinning, swirling through the air. She watched them flit and dodge, dance and collide, coming together and breaking apart *in endless motion through the mighty void*. She looked on with something like awe.

Long into the morning, the four of them stayed put until every last engine had rumbled away. Then they ventured out, blinded, dazed. As they set off, Alice slowed, letting the others walk ahead. When she felt safely behind, she turned and looked back.

Somehow she wasn't surprised to see Frank at the edge of the copse. Nor was she surprised that he hadn't called out. There he stood in his wedding suit, looking as gentle, handsome, and proud, as untarnished by life as the day they were married, and she raised an arm, her heart smote by joy. Joy that flamed into the air, filling the woods, the universe. Then Frank did something strange. With lips pursed, he bent his knees and leapt into the air, and all that heat went cold.

In that moment there were any number of things she didn't know. For instance, that she would survive the day. That the four of them would make their way to the banks of the Yangtze River and push their way through water cannons onto a British steamer. That Old Chang would slip and fall in the chaos and never be seen again. She didn't know that she would lie in an iron hold for five days without so much as matting until they reached Wuhan, or that from there they would go on another two hundred miles by train to Changsha, where with ether and an episiotomy she would give birth to a son at the hands of a stranger. Neither did she know that by the time they reached Hong Kong the whole world would be descended into madness, nor that the Japanese would take on the British too, not one month after she set sail for home. She didn't know that China would eventually win, or that after the war she would vote for the first time, or that one day her only grandchild, a girl, would play soccer on King's College Circle and walk in cap and gown through Convocation Hall in Toronto, just like her grandfather. She didn't know that one day she would see her great-grandchildren through a magic portal she could hold in her hands, and she didn't know that in the end her ashes would be scattered over the Huangpu River, which curled like a hairpin through the heart of Shanghai, the last place she had been truly happy, though life would not be without happiness, as far as happiness went.

And she didn't know if she believed in God or the afterlife. All she knew, what she finally came to accept, was that the sweet, inimitable assemblage of atoms that was Frank Yeung was no more. And indeed, when she looked again, he was gone.

PATRICK DOERKSEN

LEECH

Why do Mom and Dad shut their door every night? Liz says they do. I haven't seen it. I go to bed too early. I wonder if they have one too, coming after them. I wonder if they know a door can't stop it?

I've never thought that maybe everyone has one. If Liz has one it would be something with wings. Liz spends all day with her friends in the tree fort. She likes to jump from the high dive at the pool. She says if she had one super power she would choose to fly.

If I had a superpower I would fly too, but for different reasons.

Mom and Dad are in the military. It's nothing to do with guns and bombs. Actually, it's more boring than even being a plumber. I watched the plumber last week fix the sink. He seemed much happier than Dad. Dad's behind a desk and sometimes he doesn't talk to anybody at all for a whole day, except on the phone. Mom's behind a desk too, but she's the opposite, all day she's talking to people. She's a chaplain. That's probably just as boring.

In the military you always have someone telling you what to do. Mostly they tell Mom and Dad to move here, now move there. We've moved twice in the past four years. This is great for me, it keeps me away from it. I don't like to think what will happen when we stop moving. Liz hates moving, but maybe she should be grateful if she also has one.

I dreamed last night about a forest of bonsai. Bonsai are trees shrunken by a laser beam so that people can put them in their house. I don't really believe that, but how else do they get so small? Dad says he has a friend with a shrink ray, and now we have a bonsai in the bathroom. I like to imagine an owl got caught sleeping when they shrunk the tree and woke up tiny and now lives on the sow bugs behind the toilet. In my dream I was walking in the bonsai forest trying not to break the trees. It turned out the whole world had become a bonsai. I could see everywhere, over mountains even, like I was looking at a map, and I could see it coming toward me.

That's not so different from what I imagine during the day though. When we're in a circle and Mrs. Schulz is reading I look out the window and am afraid it's there moving along the fence. A couple nights ago I imagined it wriggling through the muck beneath a river somewhere miles and miles away. It's something like a slug or a leech, shot out from some weird place in the ground, or maybe from space.

It's very slow, and that's my only hope. It takes an afternoon to cross a road, a year to cross a state. But it's still scary because it never stops moving. It's not annoyed by buildings or lakes or anything in its way, it just keeps going. It doesn't need to sleep or eat. I don't know where it gets its energy from. Everything needs energy to keep it moving. Maybe there are things that don't? Maybe it's not doing the moving, maybe it's being pulled, reeled into me like a fish.

I'm not sure what happens if it catches me. I used to have nightmares of falling into a pit of leeches.

Something like that, I'm guessing.

I tried to explain this to Mom. She just kept asking me why I was so sure.

But I'm not sure. I can't be sure. So sometimes when I've been playing for too long with LEGO in the basement, or reading too long under the trampoline, I need to get up and go somewhere else, just in case.

Today Mom did something she'd never done before. She brought back a map and a big sheet of paper from work and spread it over the kitchen table.

Where did you see it last, she said.

When we were camping by the lake near Grandma and Grandpa's, I said.

It's summertime and I do a lot of exploring. I collect things. I was climbing a tree to get this huge pinecone when I thought I saw it across the lake.

How long would it take to get from the fridge to where I'm standing, Mom said.

Half an hour, I said.

Mom wrote all this down on the paper. I stood on my tiptoes watching her write down numbers and cross out numbers. Eventually she circled one big number at the bottom.

I've calculated it out, she said. From the lake to us it will take a year and three months. I looked at the paper but it was just a bunch of numbers.

Are you sure, I said.

I've used math, she said, and math is the surest thing in the world.

I'm not sure I saw it at the lake, I said.

Mom grabbed up the paper with the numbers and crunched it into the garbage. She was mad.

I'm sorry, I said. I didn't know she was going to do all that work. She had her hands all tangled up in her hair.

The only sure thing is that it always moves toward me, I said.

She sat down at the table then and told me to sit down too.

I want you to imagine something for me, Hans, she said. Imagine it showing up right here in our kitchen, right there on the floor where the carpet becomes tiles. It's so slow, you could leap right over it! You could even tap dance around it if you wanted!

I'd be too scared, I said.

Then I'd help you scoop it up into a box and ship it to Africa, she said.

When it arrived there it would just start crawling back toward me, it wouldn't even be angry, I said.

We could send it into space, she said.

No we couldn't, I said.

We could confuse it, she said. Maybe it was tracking me by my hair, maybe we could cut off my hair and send it to Uncle Bernie out east and make it go there?

But we can't confuse it, I said.

The only way we could confuse it would be if I died. I didn't say this though. It was a new thought.

———

Last night Mom and Dad were yelling with their door closed. I only know because I couldn't sleep, I was thinking the new thought again. I was thinking that maybe if I did kill myself it would finally get annoyed. But when I try to imagine it out there, growing slack and stopping under some rock, not moving at all, I can't. It's like it needs me. To be itself. It would be like if a rock were falling and suddenly the whole earth disappeared and the rock was left with nowhere to fall.

Is this what would really happen? I feel weird when I think about it, because I can never know. It's set up that way. If I die I won't be able to watch what happens, but if I don't die nothing different will happen.

Today Liz told me that we were going to live with Grandma and Grandpa for a while. Five minutes later, Mom told me the same thing.

I'm really scared. Mom didn't make any calculations for that. It would reach me much quicker, I can't say how quick, but a lot quicker, since I saw it out there when we went camping. I told Mom that I wasn't going. She just hugged me and kissed me again and again on my forehead.

Please, Mom, what should I do, I said. I was crying. Mom was crying too.

I'm laying a spell on you, she said. She was still kissing me.

What does the spell do, I said.

It's so that it can't touch you, not for a moment, she said. If you see it, if it comes to your door when you're in bed, don't be scared.

How long will the spell last, I said.

Two days, she said.

That's not very long, I said.

It's the best I got, she said. But I will renew it every two days. I will never let it expire.

I've been at Grandma and Grandpa's now for five days and I haven't seen it. Mom's come twice, Dad's come once. I'm not sure kisses are enough to stop it. I'm not sure because Mom kisses Liz too and Liz is starting to get really sick. I think hers is getting close. Everyone has one, I'm pretty sure of that now. I'm telling Mom and Dad we need to get Liz back home, we need to or something horrible will happen, but Mom and Dad don't understand, they just keep kissing us like that will make everything okay.

KELLY WARD

A GIRL AND A DOG ON A FRIDAY NIGHT

Rachel can see half of her windshield through the front window of the store, above the pile of overstuffed bright pink pigs that lines the entryway. That helps. The constant glint of sunlight prevents her from seeing inside the car, but still she oscillates between glaring at the cashier—frantically willing her to move faster—and checking the windshield. It disturbs her that with every step she takes toward the register the visible area of her car shrinks behind the behemoth cab of a pickup parked next to her sedan.

On a wire rack beside her, a few headlines call out the unseasonably low temperatures expected for the weekend. *Nineteen is still hot*, Rachel thinks. *No. Not hot. Warm.* Seeing the checkout girl's hand move to the phone next to her till and hearing her voice over the store's PA system, Rachel cringes.

"Intimates, call 202, please." A purple spangled thong hangs from the cashier's left index finger. Rachel can see that the tag clipped to the thigh reads $3.99, while the register blinks $4.99.

Honestly, I'll give her the extra dollar, Rachel thinks, training her gaze on the rail-thin woman at the front of the line, her sharp elbow straining against the pink velour of her zip-up as she leans against the conveyor belt, one hand perched on a bony hip.

The pickup has been replaced by a massive SUV and Rachel's car is now completely blocked from view. She thinks she might see someone standing next to her car through the tinted glass of the SUV. Above her, banks of fluorescent lights give the store a sickly, bluish hue, even from twenty feet above. *A hand lifting a phone to an ear? Is that a baseball cap? Maybe just the guy who owns the truck. Too hot for him to make a call from the driver's seat? Goddamn it.*

The cashier continues to speak into her handset. The velour-suited woman has purchased an assortment of items that can only be amassed at a giant store such as this: sequined thong, enormous bag of dog food, tube of glittery lip gloss. Teeth sucking and sighs are beginning to rise from the line of customers. Rachel is pretty sure she'll have the crowd on her side if she complains, but she says nothing. Squinting through the glare that bounces from the SUV's left mirror, she tries to clearly determine who it is that's standing next to her car. She looks for the silhouette of a brow, the profile of a jaw. She is most concerned that it is a woman. *A woman who thinks that dogs should be outfitted with water-dispensing backpacks six months out of the year. That'd be my luck.* The snark of her own thoughts makes Rachel feel a little ill. *You know you shouldn't have left them in there.* Betsy is probably a bit of a grey area. Not a lot of fur. Used to being outside all summer. But Betsy isn't the only one in the car.

Luca had screamed when Rachel tried to unbuckle her seat belt. Arched her back so that her rib cage pulled tight against her pink Superman T-shirt and pressed her white-knuckled fists into Rachel's chest.

"I'm not going! Not going!" she'd said, baring her teeth in primal defiance. As soon as Rachel had finally given up and let her fall back into the well-worn cradle of her booster seat, red-faced and breathless, she'd added, "Get me a Rolo, Mom?"

With no additional cashier in sight, no movement in the line, and the disturbingly consistent whir of the store's air conditioning in her ears, Rachel can't move her eyes from the front window of the store. She can make out the hood of her sedan. For a moment it looks as if she had imagined the figure standing beside her car, phone to ear. There's no movement beyond the flash of a slight shadow over the blue hood. The plastic clatter of the cashier's phone finally finding its way back to its hook brings her focus back into the store. The underwear are quickly bagged and the bra beneath the velour hoodie is awkwardly adjusted as the entire line waits for APPROVED to appear on the debit machine screen. As the girl at the front of the line pulls her card out, something catches Rachel's eye.

Another shadow. Short this time, and hovering over the hood of her car. Getting longer. A body in movement toward the nose of the sedan. Finally she comes into view. A woman, maybe forty, forty-five, her bleached blond hair piled high in a messy topknot. Rachel watches as she moves to the front of the car, phone still to her ear. The woman looks back and forth from the plate to the windshield, her eyes pinched at the corners, her head just barely shaking.

Shit.

The wire shopping basket hits the floor with more clatter than Rachel would have liked. She runs to the automatic door too quickly and she waits—face an inch from the glass—for it to open enough to slip through. The heat of the day hits her, and her fright mixes with guilt and a fresher, deeper panic that has nothing to do with the stranger calling in her licence plate number. *Nineteen without the humidex. Shit.*

The keys are somehow in her hand—she doesn't remember fishing in her purse—and she is shoving them into the driver's-side-door lock before the woman in front of the car can say a word—won't look until the ignition has been turned.

"Hey. What are you doing? You left your kid in there. It's practically sweltering out. Don't—hey!"

Rachel is in the driver's seat and the door is somehow closed beside her. The keys won't find the ignition. She pulls her hand back and tries again.

"I called you in. The cops are coming and they have your plate number."

The woman is right next to the driver's-side window. She pushes a pair of bug-eyed sunglasses onto her head to look Rachel dead in the eye.

Finally Rachel leans her entire body to the right so that her face is inches from the ignition. Only then can she successfully push the key through the slot and start the engine. She doesn't look into the back seat. If she did, she thinks she might be sick. A warm lick on the back of her neck as she rights herself does little to quell her feelings of dread. Betsy's kisses are usually cool as a tomato slice. Those are Luca's words, not hers. She instinctively twists one arm behind the passenger seat to back out of the parking spot and meets Luca's shining pink face as she does. She's blinking, and flushed.

"It's kinda hot in here, Mama," Luca says.

The woman outside slaps the window as Rachel pulls away.

"I'm gonna wait here for . . ."

Rachel can't hear the end of the sentence over the AC fan, but she is pretty sure she gets the gist. The traffic light just outside the parking lot is red, so she makes a right just to keep moving.

"Betsy thinks I should get two Popsicles when we get home," Luca says as she presses one finger against the glass next to her. "And she'd like to chew the sticks when I'm done, please and thank you."

Rachel drives for ten minutes in whatever direction will put the most distance between her and the mega-mart store in the shortest span of time. She finally stops at a rusty little parkette.

Two of the four swings hang limp and unslung from their chains, but the two that still cling to their hinges are enough to send Luca swirling toward the set, arms pinwheeling as if she were directing some uncontrollable orchestra. Betsy bounds around her, bowing and jumping as they go. Rachel thought there would be absolution in seeing them play and run freely, proof that she has done them no permanent harm. But that doesn't come. Relief perhaps, but guilt nonetheless. Luca leaps onto a swing, trusting the fraying canvas to catch her weight. Betsy is cautious as ever. She is just careful enough so that Luca will keep playing with her, keep loving her. The two of them, Luca and Betsy, have that in common. A calculated manipulation that comes from a place of total innocence.

Rachel pulls her phone from her pocket. She unlocks it, sliding her thumb slower than usual over the greasy screen. She knows she has not missed any calls; the side of her abdomen where the phone rests in the kangaroo pouch of her hoodie is acutely attuned to its vibrations. But she hopes. Maybe in her panic at the store she's missed a text, email, something, from Travis. Nothing.

Their last conversation had been exactly seven hours ago. Rachel was on the way home from picking up Luca at the community centre—where she had spent three hours chasing soft red balls around a gym and sitting in a circle singing songs she didn't know the words to. Rachel was sure there was more to it than that, but those two activities seemed to be the only ones Luca ever remembered participating in.

"How was Little School, Lu?" Rachel would ask as they rushed through the brown-tiled hallway of the community centre. "Little School" was Luca's name for the community centre daycare program. It was where she spent three days a week before Long School, a.k.a. kindergarten.

"Same. Sang a song."

"Oh, yeah, what song?"

"How would I know?"

Rachel arranged her lunch breaks on Mondays, Wednesdays, and Fridays to coincide with shuttling Luca between the community centre and school. It was a tense trip that saw Rachel lead-footing through every just barely red light she came across and whipping glances between the speedometer and the rear-view mirror, constantly fearful she'd see flashing lights behind her. Travis should have known not to call between noon and one on a Friday. At least Rachel thought he should have known. So she ignored the first buzz of her phone against her rib cage. Telemarketer, she figured. Or their landlord calling about the next six months' worth of rent cheques. It buzzed a second time just as Rachel was attempting a left-hand turn into the school parking lot through a not-quite-wide-enough gap in the steady flow of midday traffic. An oncoming pickup sped up for dramatic effect while blasting its horn directly into Luca's ears in her passenger's-side booster seat.

"Loud much?" Luca had said, turning her face full and defiant toward the approaching silver grill.

Rachel swung into the closest open parking spot and pulled the phone from her pocket. She nearly tossed it against her cheek.

"Hello? Yeah, hello?"

"Hey. You sound like you're running. What's going on?"

"Jeezus. You know I'm in the middle of driving Lu, why are you calling me now? Hold on a sec."

Rachel reached into the back seat and pre-emptively unclasped Luca's seat belt. She dropped the phone on the driver's seat as she shuffled around the car—her work heels make running impossible—to the passenger's-side back door. She lifted Luca from her seat and swung her onto one hip. Luca would soon be too heavy for this manoeuvre. Rachel resolved to try lifting weights to delay that reality. Once Luca was required to move around on her own, the pace of Rachel's life would slow to an unlivable crawl.

The period bell was ringing just as Rachel plopped Luca in front of the classroom door. The door itself was split in half widthwise so that adults could see into and out of the classroom, but students were kept inside by an impassable four-foot barrier. All the children sat on a red carpet at the rear of the room, save one chubby little girl with stringy blond hair who stood in the middle of the room on her tip-toes trying to see over the half door to catch a glimpse of who it was that was arriving after the bell. Rachel reached over the door to unlatch it and guided Luca into the room. Luca didn't look back as Rachel kissed the top of her head before closing the door behind her. Rachel made a mental note to find out why Luca's hair smelled like peanut butter as she sprint-shuffled to her car, almost turning her heel as she tried to jump the loose metal threshold on the door to the playground.

"Hey, okay, sorry, I had to get Luca into school."

Rachel was breathless as she clambered back behind the wheel and started the car.

"Dude, this is long distance," Travis said. "You could have just said 'Call me back.'"

"Whatever. I'm in the middle of something here. You know I have a whole routine."

"I'm standing at a pay phone with a line of six guys behind me." Travis lowered his voice. "I had to pretend I was still talking to you that entire time so they wouldn't get pissed."

Rachel laughed. "What did you say?"

"They think you have a prescription drug problem now. It started with me pretending I couldn't hear you, then you were high, then we fought about you taking out prescriptions in my name. It was the best I could think of on the spot."

"We are more than even for me leaving you on hold then."

A yellow light in front of her, Rachel decided to stop. It was good to hear Travis's voice.

"Hey, so listen," he said, his tone straightening a little, as it did when he had something practised to say. Rachel noticed the change but ignored it.

"Ohmigod, it's, like, twelve-thirty, aren't you supposed to be on your way to the airport?" she interrupted.

"Yeah, that's the thing." His tone remained rigid, unmistakably so. "So, Deluth has a double he needs somebody to work, a straight turnover between night shift and afternoon today."

"Okay . . ."

"So I'm gonna do it. Since it's overtime it'll be time and a half, and it'll be a full shift. Nine hours."

"Okay, so you're gonna come home tomorrow, then?"

"Well, that's the thing," Travis said again. Everything was "the thing" when Travis tried to convince Rachel of something. It is among her top five pet-peeve phrases. Along with "no-brainer" and "slam dunk" (when not used in a strictly basketball-related context).

"The shift runs from four till one, so I'll get back to my bunk around two. I'll need to sleep off the double shift, and then get cleaned up and packed, so by the time I'd be ready to come home, the only flight would be a red eye, and then there would kinda be no point."

A small, nauseating quiver shot up Rachel's spine, but she did not speak. Having a relationship that consisted solely of phone conversations for five days a week, inflection, intonation, and phraseology had become incredibly important to her. She hated the way Travis built his sentences like scaffolding around his point. Language was never a bridge for him, something that linked his thoughts to her understanding by a straight and sturdy route. His speech reminded her of the planks she'd once nailed to the dying pine tree in her parents' backyard, trying to fashion a ladder when she was too weak to climb it. Like those planks, Travis's words spiraled round and round, looking sound enough at first glance. But as soon as Rachel tried to rely on them, they all came loose.

"So, bottom line is, you're not coming home."

"Well, don't say it like that! I don't have a choice."

"Yes, you do. Just say you can't do the double. What am I supposed to do with Lu? I have stuff I gotta do. There's . . . just, stuff. And I don't do it during the week because I know I'll be able to do it when you're home."

"Yeah, I know, but Duluth is already gone. He had his brother's wedding or something last night, and when he asked me I'd already had a couple, and I didn't know what to say."

"You've known since when, then?"

"What do you mean?"

"Since Wednesday, then? If he had his brother's wedding last night?"

"Well, yeah."

"And I talked to you on Wednesday night. And you were drunk. So you must have talked to Duluth before you talked to me."

"Jeezus. I don't know. I guess."

Rachel looked out over the steering wheel. Her left arm was looped through it backward, so that her fingernails were hooked over the top, facing her. She had been anticipating a turn. She suddenly realized that she needed to do her nails. The matte, powder-blue polish on her index finger was chipping and she could see the flaky ridges of the brittle nail beneath.

"Hello?"

Rachel said nothing.

"This call is really expensive. So if you're not gonna talk, I'm—"

"Yeah, okay. I gotta go anyway. I'm driving."

"Kay."

"Kay."

She slipped her thumb onto the red circle on her screen without even moving the phone from her cheek.

A muffled thumping follows Rachel and Luca as they wind their way from the park to home. Rachel rolls up her window in an effort to stifle the sound. She knows it is coming from somewhere within the engine of the Honda, but she is convinced that if it can be made inaudible it can't be bad enough for a trip to the mechanic. But the metallic drumming can still be heard through the closed window; and over the whine of Christina Aguilera through the speakers; and over the whir of the fan through the vents. Rachel exhales and rolls her eyes. She has always been a champion eye roller, even without an audience. It's automatic. Symptomatic. Like a cough or a sneeze, the unique sound a person makes when they first sit down after a day spent on their feet. There will be no trips to the mechanic until Travis is back to deal with it.

In the rear-view mirror she watches Luca as she considers the city, block by block, fence post by fence post, as it passes her window. Rachel can see her eyes twitch as they try to focus on the moving objects. For a second Rachel wonders if Travis notices things like that. When he decided to take a job that would put two provinces between him and Luca 80 per cent of the time, he had told Rachel it would be good for them.

Make the time he did spend with her more fun. "I'll be home on weekends, so I'll be here for all the good stuff." Somehow he seemed to forget that left Rachel with the bad stuff.

The last weekend he was home, while Rachel made dinner for the three of them, he'd taken Luca to the park near their apartment. Just a little grass square with one swing set and a free-standing, rust-rimmed metal slide. Luca returned riding high and hands-free on Travis's shoulders. Rachel watched them from the living room window as Travis spun down the street, taking two steps forward and then spinning in place three hundred and sixty degrees, dipping his head from side to side to let Luca flop and sway this way and that. In the two strides forward, Luca would catch her breath, clasping fistfuls of hair from the top of Travis's head. Then, just before the spin, she tossed her arms above her head, her fingers spread wide and joyous, blue sky breaking between them as he sent her swirling. It was a level of physical wonder Rachel would never be able to recreate. She didn't have the height, nor the stomach, needed to twirl Luca with seeming abandon over concrete and asphalt and know that she would not be dropped.

Travis's love was huge and grand. It was an obvious kind of love Rachel assumed any child craved. She watched them walking for half a block, taking a full seven minutes to cover a hundred and fifty metres of sidewalk. When the front door finally swung open, Luca was already in full sprint toward Rachel.

"Did you see me flying?" she squealed, leaping with her arms outstretched toward Rachel.

Rachel caught her under the arms, but the heavy force of her momentum and her growing weight meant that the leap resulted in a feeble little half spin, and then Luca was grounded again.

"Daddy's a lot stronger," Luca said, hands on her hips.

She ran through the wide doorway toward the kitchen, where Travis stood arched over the open fridge door. Luca ducked under his arm and stood staring up into his face.

"Hey, Lu."

In the rear-view Rachel can see that Luca hasn't taken her eyes off the window. A man walking three miniature pinschers passes by and Luca actually swivels in her seat, straining her cheek against the glass to watch the stumps of their little docked tails jutting straight up toward the overcast sky.

"Lu? Hello? Mom to Lu. Are you there?"

Luca waits until the dogs have rounded a corner before slowly turning her head. "Um-hmm?" she hums, looking Rachel straight in the eyes through the mirror.

In that look Rachel sees a glimpse of the teenage self Luca will become—it is both amusing and terrifying.

"How about we swing by the park again after dinner?"

Luca turns back toward the window, shrugging her shoulders.

To enter their apartment, Rachel must drive down the laneway between their house and the neighbour's. The boxy little sedan nearly skims the brick on either side as she manoeuvres around two sets of trash bins. Clear of the laneway, she makes a tight left onto the wavy patch of gravel that serves as a parking spot. The yard of the house is enclosed in chain-link on three sides, the open side running directly parallel to the length of the car.

Rachel throws the car into park, grabs her purse from the floor of the back seat, and unbuckles Luca's seat belt with one

deep lean between the front seats. Luca is dexterous enough
to scramble out and pop open the door once the criss-cross of
buckles has been unlocked. Betsy leaps out after her, clearing
the booster seat completely and landing on the gravel. They
skip around to the back of the car. In the rear-view Rachel can
see the fuzzy purple spray of Luca's scrunchy over the lip of
the trunk. She stays in the driver's seat for a moment, listening
to the intermittent pings of the cooling engine. The dash
clock reads seven thirty-two. Sixty-two hours before she'll
walk Luca back into morning snack time at the community
centre. She hears Luca in the tiny, almost-fenced yard running up and down the wooden steps of the apartment door.

"Up, up, up, and I'm a king in the castle. Down, down,
down, and I'm drowning in the moat."

Through the loose faux leather of her purse, Rachel feels her
phone vibrate. Not long enough to be a call, so she knows it
cannot be Travis. A spam text, reading, "IMPORTANT MESSAGE:
your mobile number has been identified as part of a massive
online banking breach. To confirm your account is secure, call
this number back immediately." The number is international,
at least fourteen digits long. The whole thing doesn't fit in the
little box at the top of the message. Rachel texts back as she gets
out of the car, "Should I jus send u my visa number and bank
account login now to save myself the long distance? Asshole."

"Lu, let's go," she calls to Luca, who is bent next to the
fence, her face inches above some grass Betsy is chewing. She
turns her head toward Rachel without righting her body.

"Now, guys, come on."

Luca skates across the grass, not lifting her pink boots from
the ground, and lets her arms swing stiffly at her sides.

"Speed skater," Luca says in a mockingly deep man's voice.

Betsy takes another pull from the crabgrass and jumps up onto the mouldy decking without using the stairs, careful to avoid landing on the one rotting, grey board.

Inside the kitchen the steel of the door is cool against Rachel's forehead. She leans against it as she toes her shoes and kicks them onto the heap next to the door. She pivots on her forehead to face the kitchen. Dishes piled high and dried just enough to make scrubbing futile. And beyond, in the dining room, Luca's scrambled mess of crayons and construction paper. She can't see Luca, but she can hear her in her bedroom, the springs of her mattress straining under what may well be her last round of jumping. Betsy has her front paws up on the edge of the Formica dining table, her head tilted to the side, straining to grab a red crayon in her jaws. Rachel doesn't stop her. She won't relish dabbing up the inevitable bloody-looking vomit hours from now, but she's not in the mood to raise her voice to the level it would take to stop her. Her purse buzzes again.

"You're kidding me," she says as she taps open a text from the same long-distance number.

"Yes ok. texting details is fine. We will make sure your account is secure."

Betsy's nails make one final, digging pull to lunge her lips toward her prize. As soon as she has it she scrambles into Luca's room, the metallic crunching of the mattress getting louder, and more frayed with each leap. Then silence. And a barely audible "Oops."

They finish up a late meal of Kraft Dinner and hot dogs, and Rachel shuffles Luca from the table into her pyjamas, with some cajoling, and finally onto her now broken bed with one duct-taped spring.

"I wanna play space when Daddy gets home."

Luca says this not with excitement or glee, but with the stern look of someone making their final offer after a terse negotiation. She will tolerate nothing less than playing "space," which means sitting on the steps of the porch and leaning back so that the roofs of the four houses that surround their little scrap of backyard form a perfect frame through which to travel to the stars. Forget that most of the "stars" are actually overnight flights or the odd satellite. This is one of many games that only Travis is permitted to play with Luca. Early in the summer, when the long days meant no lights could be seen in the sky before 10 p.m. Rachel had tried to soothe Luca to sleep by suggesting they play space. Luca's bedroom was sweltering, nearly forty degrees, Rachel figured, when she opened the door to find her lying starfished on top of her duvet, her sweaty head flopped sideways toward the door.

"I need some water, Ma. I'm dying in here," Luca had said before flinging both legs up into the air and back down onto the mattress with a loud huff. Rachel gave her a drink that was 60 per cent ice and carried her out onto the porch to cool off. The only fan in the house rattled from the kitchen ceiling, so she left the back door open with the fan whirring at top speed. It was enough to move the air a little bit on the porch, on an otherwise completely breezeless night, Rachel put Luca on the step and leaned her elbows back against the prickly wood.

"Are we ready for liftoff, captain?" Rachel whispered, mimicking the lines she had heard Travis use. Luca didn't respond. She craned her face up toward the sky.

"We're headed to Orion's Belt this mission, right, captain?"

Still no response. She looked down and took a sip of water.

"Captain, I need the okay to start the engines."

Luca looked up at Rachel, hair matted across her forehead in wet, sweeping strings. Luca pushed it aside, giving her head the distinct look of a middle-aged comb-over.

"We can't play space, Ma. You don't sound like a spaceman."

"Well, you don't sound like a spaceman either. Just use your imagination."

"No. You gotta have one real spaceman at least. That's the rule."

Luca took another sip from her cup, then stood. She leaned in and hugged the top of Rachel's head, then shimmied off into the house to fall asleep on the cool bathroom floor.

Telling Luca that there was no chance she would be playing space this weekend might permanently derail the evening— send Luca into a tight-lipped rage. Rachel looks at her daughter, who is propped with her hands outstretched behind her, her brow scrunched into an impossibly deep furrow.

"Maybe another time," Rachel says, leaving the news that Travis won't be coming home unbroken for the time being. She'll tell her tomorrow. Or not at all. She doesn't want to see Luca's disappointment. She's tired of seeing it. And the fact that she's tired of it makes her feel even worse.

Rachel leaves Luca on the bed, sitting bolt upright, singing a song to Betsy as she holds the ends of Betsy's soft limp ears between her fingers and makes them dance.

Outside, the night is breezy but still warm. Rachel drops herself onto the top step of the porch and digs her elbows into her knees. A bat darts between the big maple that stands just beyond the rusted-out Honda and an evergreen in the neighbour's yard. She wonders what else lives in that tree. Whether it is full of its own dramatic life of feuds and turf wars and angling for leaf and trunk space. She doesn't marvel at the thought. It feels futile. Kind of sad. A song begins to drift through the upstairs neighbour's window. The first three words are curses before a deep bass and drum line take over.

Another bat shoots out from the canopy of the maple, this one followed by a small bird that twists around it, pecking and flapping madly. The fight continues into the neighbouring evergreen and out again into the darkness until Rachel can no longer see them.

The summer Rachel nailed up those seven-inch lengths of board on the bare and knobby pine in her parents' backyard, she'd used some thin little one-inch screws and a rubber hammer she'd found on her father's tool bench. Rachel knew that screws were not meant to be hammered, but she thought if she hit hard enough and for long enough they'd go in. And they did. A bit. But she didn't have the strength to hammer them deep enough into the dense wood of the tree to support her weight. When she tried the climb anyway, she made it to the third board before a screw popped and the spinning piece of wood sent her ass to grass.

She remembers sitting there, post-fall, looking up at the gnarled bark, the untouched boards looking firm and sturdy yet completely useless.

I'll have to teach myself how to use a drill, she thought.

MARIA REVA

SUBJECT WINIFRED

KEY COMPONENTS OF REPORT

1. *DIONAEA MUSCIPULA*

I'm disappointed to learn carnivorous plants haven't been observed to digest anything bigger than a monkey. My idea for a science-fair exhibit isn't as exciting anymore, though I don't know where I would've found the monkey or anything bigger anyway. Lisa Ferrell picked the same exhibit topic as me so I need to beat her out. It'll be an uphill battle, Lisa Ferrell's mom works in faraway places like the Amazon and that's how she gets her steady supply of seedlings. I have to settle for the ones Klaus gives me. Cradled in moist tissue paper, the seedlings are pale, wrinkly, and, as I can already see, unfit to survive.

2. GOD

Usually my mother, Winnie, sits on the front porch, smoking her Marlboros and mumbling about the president or prices or the old holly tree that keeps dropping needle leaves on the yellow lawn, but this evening she's not home so I know something is up.

I'm planting the seedlings in yogurt containers when Winnie bursts into the house. She stands at the doorway, kicks off her shoes. Sweaty and flushed, she tells me she went to the library to look for night classes and, instead, found God.

I ask, Did someone sell Him to you out of a van?

Last time she came home kicking her shoes off so energetically was when she bought a cheap Walkman from a guy in a Salvation Army parking lot. He promised it would change her life. The Walkman played half of our *Toys in the Attic* tape and ate the rest.

Don't be silly, says Winnie, this is completely different. God isn't one of those things people can sell you. There was an informational stand and she was the one who came to them.

PLACES

1. CLOSET DOOR

In my room there is a closet with a door and the inside of the door is covered in tallies and numbers. I read them every night. I have woken up 4745 times since birth, my nails grow at a rate of 1 millimetre per week (rate increasing), the moon is in Day 2 of its cycle, I have an average of 180 wake-ups until my first cycle, my exhibit will grow mouths in 5 to 7 days, Winnie is 39, Winnie has discovered herself 4 times through anonymous groups, walk-in clinics, men and women whose voices boom over crowds in need of saving. I slide a piece of chalk out of a sock, find a space between the tallies, and write: Winnie's relationship with God, number of days: 1.

2. EDISON MIDDLE SCHOOL

White wooden fencing keeps the children in. Lisa Ferrell stands in the middle of the schoolyard: sunny orange curls, alive, visible, a pretty girl with mean eyes and an upper lip too short to cover her front teeth. Between her palms, Lisa Ferrell holds a secret. She says she's not supposed to show anyone, this thing in her hands is illegal in forty-five states and can wipe out a population. Everyone stands back a little. I inch closer through the crowd. Lisa Ferrell spreads her fingers to reveal a clump of dirt wrapped in tinfoil. Tiny purple leaves stick out with hairy mouths shaped like half moons—one of her famous Venus flytraps, *Dionaea muscipula*. Lisa Ferrell's best friend unzips her Ziploc bag and tears a piece of luncheon meat off her sandwich. When Lisa Ferrell gives the nod, the best friend brushes the meat across one of the plant's open mouths. Slowly the jaws move, the teeth clench. An eighth grader claps, a kid I've never seen before claps (new?), the whole schoolyard claps as my stomach boils into my throat. I can't help thinking about my yogurt containers. My plants are showing some promising buds but still look as threatening as grass.

I imagine Lisa Ferrell in an orange uniform, which makes me feel better. That's what the girls at Nifty Finds Hardware Store have to wear forever and ever, after they fail their science-fair exhibits. She'd have to tie her hair up too, so those sunny curls don't get caught in the machinery.

3. NIFTY FINDS

Winnie used to work at Nifty Finds. She told me the uniforms used to be swamp green and made the Nifty Finds girls look jaundiced under the lamp displays until someone high up in management opted for the cheery, uppity orange. The store used to be called Thrifty Finds before the T burned out, followed by the H and R. The ifty seemed foreboding and, after all, the people in charge wanted to attract a sophisticated crowd into Edison, the Mr. Smiths and Thompsons and Browns, so they took a loopy leftover N out of storage and secured it in front. Winnie says that even though the place sucked her soul and hooked her on nicotine (the girls got away with extra breaks if they smoked), there were good moments. Good people too. I think that's how she met her Mr. Brown (Secret Number 2, see below), and I think that's how I was born. Stories come in pieces with Winnie, and I never get a full one. But I hear her whisper his name sometimes, chant it, when she sits on the front porch with her Marlboros.

4. HOUSE ON KIDD ROAD

Chicken wire keeps the dogs out. Cracks in the stucco walls: the stucco shimmers but so do the cracks because there are ants in them. And there are people in the rooms. Many, many people, now. Winnie floats around her new friends, neck and wrists wrapped in beads, shooting me looks whenever I do something sacrilegious like set up fly traps or use the microwave to cook an egg.

Today they gather around the kitchen table. They share meditation and fasting stories. They shift reality with positive thoughts. Some of them look at me or maybe something behind me or just in my general direction. They have this way of looking at you and not looking at you at the same time.

I hoist myself up onto a counter and sit with my legs hanging down, resisting the urge to swing them back and forth. With my faded khaki jacket, I blend in with the cupboards.

Among the people sitting below is a man with bright white teeth and a cleft chin. He says he used to be a high-school teacher, a real good one, until he got laid off and told he wasn't really laid off but given an opportunity to grow. He must've taken the advice to heart because all he's talking about is growing and growing. He takes a shapeless Plasticine thing out of his pocket and the others lean in a little. It's my chewing device, he says, a real lifesaver, because after all those raw food smoothies my jaw muscles started getting weak.

Awful when that happens, says a woman beside him.

Everyone nods in a moment of silence. Near silence. Their seashell necklaces shake and jingle as they nod.

When I slide off the counter, my foot gets caught in a purse strap. A woman turns to me and asks, What's your name, treasure? She offers me a bracelet made of wolf fangs and I say, Thanks but I'm really more of a cat person, which she considers with a grave face before turning back to the others.

SECRETS

1. THE HAND

Sometimes when I wake up in the morning there's a warm, unmoving hand on me. The hand is mine, but in those first precious seconds, two or three at the most, the hand feels like someone else's. I lift the sleeping arm, heavy, solid, and let the fingers slide across my cheeks, eyelids, the downy lobes of my ears, rounding my shoulders into the caress. It's all I can do before the game is up, the pain and prickling take over, and the fusion begins, as it always does.

2. MR. BROWN, P.O. BOX 450, MIAMI, FL

Once a month Mr. Brown, P.O. Box 450, Miami, FL, makes his way to Ms. Winifred Haze, 15 Kidd Road, Edison, WA, in the form of a cheque: *To cover essential amenities.* Nothing is said about Mr. Brown, at least nothing beyond those whispers, escaping her mouth like smoke.

II

METHODS & OBSERVATIONS

Wake-ups since birth: 4755. Science-fair exhibit: T-29 days. Winnie's relationship with God, number of days: 10. Winnie's new social life, number of friends: 6. Mrs. Thompson's nervous tic during Social Studies, total number of elbow twitches: approaching infinity.

Winnie is on her determined way to self-improvement and now smokes Marlboro Lights instead of Regulars. I sit beside her on the front porch, catching flies between my palms and stuffing them into killing jars. Winnie closes her eyes and breathes out a long cloud of smoke, looks at me and my flies (number of flies: 6), and decides it's a good moment to talk some more about God.

God is Energy, she says in a slow, hushed way, as if every word is heavy and final and deserves a capital, like the name of a town or continent. Imagine Feeding on His Energy, she continues. Soon I Will Feed on His Energy and Cleanse. Isn't that Nice?

I keep my face straight, mimic her voice. You Are Nuts.

Winnie rolls her eyes and I break into a giggle. She lights another Marlboro Light and tells me her entire system is poisoned, can't I see that, Poisoned, and she will start her twenty-one-day water fast soon and they say it does Wonders and she's finally getting all her thoughts in order, so how about we let go of our judgment?

I scoop a few flies out of my jar and blow them at Winnie. They stick to her woolly sweater. Her mouth hangs open but her words blur around me as I jump up and spin in circles across the porch and into my room and into my closet where the tallies slice the world into small, digestible bits.

Wake-ups since birth: 4758. Science-fair exhibit: T-26 days. Winnie's relationship with God, number of days: 13. Growth of plants, millimetres per day: 0.5. Chance of winning science fair, percentage: 0.000000000000000000000000001.

My exhibit still hasn't grown any mouths. Extra moss hasn't worked. Rainwater hasn't worked. The specially choreographed please-grow-a-tooth dance hasn't worked, though it did scare the neighbour's dog from lifting its leg at our fence ever again. I even wiped the dust off my window to let in more light. Nothing.

The smell of lemon meringue pie wafts into my room. Its homey fingers pull me into the kitchen, seat me on the countertop. Winnie and her friends are cleaning the kitchen and throwing out the contents of the fridge. The smell comes from the aerosol foam Winnie sprays over the cherry-pattern tiles, her movements quick and angry, as if the cracked little squares did something wrong.

After they empty the fridge they move on to the shelves and cupboards, all in preparation for Winnie's fast. A few days ago she even went off her Marlboro Lights.

Chip bags, Twinkies, TV dinners, frozen pizzas, tubs of margarine fly across the kitchen into a garbage bag. I see the items suspended in the air for an instant and imagine we're in zero gravity. I sit and watch. I turn the empty microwave on for a few seconds, to see what happens. Another few seconds. Ten seconds this time. Funny girl you have, someone says to Winnie. They are on to the cereal cupboard now. Fifteen seconds. What's left of the stale but perfectly frosted corn flakes spins through space. I'm winding the dial to 100000 seconds when Winnie tears the plug out of its socket and, saying all sorts of things not recorded here, carries the microwave to the back alley. Out of a cardboard box she fashions a sign: RADIATION (FREE).

1. THE HAND

And this time I drape the hand over my stomach, my shoulder, it's the loving hand that knows all my secrets. My, my, such smooth skin you have, I whisper. Do you lotion? Bubble bathe? Will you stay with me a while? Before someone drops a bag of needle leaves from the holly tree on you and me, before everything starts to prickle and your skin becomes my skin, your fingers my fingers, and when it's over it's just me again. Me lying here, trying not to move.

2. ME (THE GIRL)

Edison Middle School, science lab. Bottled insects, bottled eggs, bottled rodents, bottled bits of lung. Instruments not to be touched without supervision. Glass to keep the fingers out.

Klaus, the science teacher, looks at the girl seated across from him through two magnifying glasses that are his eyes. Beautiful grey watery eyes. The girl's bare legs don't touch the floor, she could swing them back and forth. But the girl keeps still as she asks the teacher about the effects of starvation on rats. That's an interesting question, says Klaus. His eyes drift toward the window, follow the movement of the clouds. There are measurables, he says. The girl likes this word, how it feels in her mouth as she asks if he could help her measure these measurables. For a special exhibit. For the science fair.

Why don't you do something more fun? Look at what Lisa Ferrell is doing with those little bean stalks of hers, hey?

She tells him the seedlings he'd given her earlier didn't have much of a chance. Please, Mr. Klaus. The girl knows she is good at saying please.

When the girl leaves the lab, she leaves with a promise: one rat, just one, not to be harmed (but harmed scientifically), and a whole lot of instruments not to be used (but used under supervision). Klaus even suggests the girl name the rat, the silly man.

Subject: Winifred Haze. Fast: Day 1. Age: 39 ¾ . Height: 5.8 feet. Weight, according to driver's licence (expired): 140 lb. Hair: brown. Eyes: blue. Smoker, nail chewer. A history of mumbling.

Subject Winifred reports feeling light. Before you bring in the new, you have to cut away the old and the sick, she says. Subject Winifred whizzes around the house, breathing easy in a cloud of euphoria and a team of supporters.

Another kitchen meeting:

I see you got rid of your microwave, says the woman sitting beside Chewing Man. A hard step but well worth it, she says. That's one less thing cooking us all in deadly invisible waves.

The woman is a Certified Breatharian, though a troubled Certified Breatharian. How am I supposed to feed on sunrays if there are none, she says. That's the problem with the West Coast. I'm pretty sure my DNA is already restructuring itself to absorb more nutrients from the air but—

For a slice of a second, light fills the kitchen. Someone gasps. Who snapped a photo? asks Chewing Man.

Subject Winifred narrows her eyes at me, tells me to go to my room.

How lovely, you didn't mention you had a child, says the Breatharian and looks in Subject Winifred's general direction. Subject Winifred hesitates between a nod and a shake so her head goes around in a lopsided circle, which makes me laugh a little. She mutters something about my born ability for cam-ouflage, and that makes me laugh too.

There's no shortage of food for me—the natural-disaster suit-case went untouched during the cleaning. Every day is a feast: canned beans, canned soup, canned spaghetti, canned meatballs, and for dessert, canned syrupy angel food cake with maraschino cherries (also canned). Two winters ago, Winnie came home dragging a cartload of food, convinced a major earthquake was coming to town that evening. Dragging, because the security feature on the cart's wheel snapped shut when she tried rolling it out of the store. Good thing she did that. Looking out for our survival, thrifty Winnie.

——

Subject: Winifred. Fast: Day 3. Weight: 134 lb. (When asked to step onto scale, Subject Winifred frowns and says, You think I'm doing this to lose weight?) A white coating on the tongue, a sweet quality to the breath. Subject Winifred leans on doorframes before passing through them. Vomits at the sight of canned feast on the table.

That's pretty normal, says Klaus when asked about the symptoms above, just the body readjusting to its new state of being. When did you see Patches throwing up, though? he asks. Patches is the name he's given the rat. I haven't seen him throwing up, Klaus says.

Today Mr. Brown, P.O. Box 450, Miami, FL, arrives in the form of a cheque with the words *Dream big and dare to fail* printed on it in gold. His cheques always have inspirational messages on them. *Constant dripping hollows out the stone. The world is all gates, all opportunities. Happiness depends upon ourselves. The going is the goal.*

III

OBSERVATIONS (CONT'D)

Subject: Winifred. Fast: Day 7. Weight: 129 lb. Enlarged eyes or the illusion of enlarged eyes?

Subject W meditates on the front porch. The neighbour's dog runs up to the chicken wire fence and barks at the wax figure in the flowing shirt but W keeps her eyes shut as she tries to see to the Real World where God and Light reside.

Yesterday Annabelle Poitras, the Certified Breatharian, said the human body is a dark house with blackened windows, and we try to look out at the real world but are aware of very little.

What does Subject W see in the Real World? Yesterday Annabelle Poitras said there are a billion colours and neons and frequencies above the normal human range of perception and hummingbird tail feathers vibrate like violin strings and—

I am trying to *meditate*, Subject W says, one eye squinting at me. I ask if she's seen the Real World yet and what does it look like.

A lot prettier than this one.

Prettier how?

Subject W closes her eye again and suggests I do something productive rather than follow her around taking pictures of her so-called natural habitat.

I am doing something productive, I say. Prettier how?

Close your eyes, she whispers.

Okay.

What do you see?

Eyelids. Nothing.

Look closer.

But—

Ssssssssh . . .

IV

SOURCES OF ERROR

Subject W is sleeping on the couch for the nineteenth hour when the girl starts to rattle her, brings can after can of food for her, eats it in front of her, tries to push a spoon of mango syrup at her mouth, one spoon of syrup please, and W opens her eyes and considers the spoon before shaking the girl off with an unknown strength. The spoon and can of syrup crash to the floor.

You scared me, W says. I'm fine! She pinches her cheeks to prove it.

The girl almost blew the entire exhibit, stupid, stupid girl.

Trying to sound smooth, the girl says she needs a nice shirt for a science fair that's coming up. Subject W asks how fancy does the shirt have to be. Pretty fancy, the girl guesses. Preferably with buttons and a front pocket. W says she happens to have the old swamp-green one from her days at ifty Finds, and it has buttons and even a front pocket, if you can believe it. And the girl thanks goodness.

I don't think Patches is doing too well, says Klaus, prodding the rat with a gloved finger. A few hairs fly off its body and glitter under the lab lamp like star dust.

Have you been keeping an eye on him? Making sure he's drinking? Haven't seen you around the lab much lately. The refeeding phase is part of the experiment too, you know. And have you seen the camera?

Klaus's words flutter by me and for a second I forget where I am. Klaus looks at me like a kid looks at a worm steamrolled into fresh asphalt. Curious but a little sorry at the same time.

Klaus asks if I want to know a fun fact. It's how he cheers up his keener students after a bad grade. Last week he told Ricky Fielder the average person weighs nine pounds post-cremation—not much more than a newborn, hey? Lisa Ferrell burst out laughing and Ricky Fielder burst into tears. Anybody who is anybody in Edison knows Ricky Fielder's the one with the troubles at home. So there was Klaus in front of thirty wide-eyed students, scouring all the shelves and drawers of his mind for another fun fact to save the day.

No thank you, I say to him and he says, I'll just go ahead and tell you anyway. I tell him I've already heard the one about the mantis shrimp and he says, Oh.

V

PHYSICAL POSSIBILITIES & IMPOSSIBILITIES

Subject: Winifred. Fast: Day 14. Weight: 115 lb. Subject W is unresponsive to sight of food. That sweet smell of the breath is acetone, according to Klaus, a toxic product of the body eating away at itself. Also a sign of kidney malfunction. Common household uses of acetone: paint thinner, nail-polish remover.

I've never felt lighter, cleaner, better, says Subject W during a kitchen meeting.

The others nod—they've all been through this before. Chewing Man fasted for eight weeks once. Annabelle Poitras for twelve. That's how she became closer to God, found eternal joy. She says in the final phase, when your body is free of toxins and your tongue is pink as a baby's, that's when you really feel it.

W says she can't wait to feel it.

You'll know when it's happening.

She'll know when it's happening.

It's like you are in a ray of colours, says Annabelle, and what you're breathing is not air but pure unadulterated energy and you want to breathe it forever. And it's warm and kind and you're gone from all the shit back here, prodding you every day, you're gone. It doesn't touch you anymore.

The others nod.

W nods.

Annabelle smiles and puts her hand on my hand. It's warm, her hand, and I should but don't move my own.

The rat died this morning. It was all gritty fur and bones at the end, like an owl pellet, whatever the bird can't digest and has to choke back out.

I'm not happy about this, not happy at all, says Klaus. His magnified eyes bore into mine and I wonder if he can see anything past them. The school administration won't like it either, he adds.

I tell him I didn't know when the refeeding phase was supposed to start.

That's why you should have been here measuring, he says. Blood pressure, body heat, urine volume—wasn't Patches your whole exhibit?

I tell him it was. I do the downcast eye and knitted brow thing heroines do in English class because at this moment I guess I'm supposed to be conflicted and heart-wrenched.

Might be a bit of my fault too, Klaus says, petting the rat's foot. Should've kept him better company. He might've just lost hope after a while. Poor Patches.

Poor Patches, says Lisa Ferrell after class. Klaus told me. That sucks.

It really is a physical impossibility for her upper lip to touch the lower one.

Don't worry about it, I say, and ask how her plants are doing. Good, big, eating up a storm, she says. Can't catch enough flies to keep up. I'm surprised your mom doesn't catch them all for you, I say, and she says, What's that supposed to mean? I say nothing. Even if my mom did catch them, Lisa Ferrell says, she'd have to mail them to me in a little envelope all the way from Saka. Saka, Madagascar. Actually, a giant envelope because the flies in Madagascar are giant. That's where my mom is now: Madagascar. Well that's just neat, I say. Lisa Ferrell deflates a little when she says, Nah, not really.

VI

THAT FOR WHICH SHE IS SORRY

Subject: Winifred. Fast: Day 21. Weight: 110 lb (estimate). Kitchen meeting attendance: 3. Science-fair exhibit: T-3 days. W is extremely prostrated, one of Klaus's favourite words. W perspires. W's interactions with the world and its mysterious workings decrease. Caught smoking a Marlboro deliciously in bed, mumbling like old times, one stem of an arm resting on layers of fleece blankets. It could be snapped between two fingers, this arm.

Honey, maybe you should try a different strategy, Annabelle whispers, rewinding her sandal straps around her ankles, about to head out the door. She's busy these days, working at a laser hair-removal clinic. Soon all the others are busy these days. The stucco house empties.

Subject W shows no desire for refeeding and will keep fasting past 21 days. Past what, exactly, she does not say.

In the next room, the girl can't sleep. Her skin is live, electric, her sheets burn. She reads her closet tallies, all of them, even the ones from the beginning of time. Their controlled, steady shapes are cool and calming as they centipede into the future. Tomorrow she will have woken up for the 4781st time. Her nails will have grown 1/5 of a millimetre. The day after tomorrow, the girl will have won.

Subject: Winifred. Fast: Day 23. Weight: unknown. Ankles swollen. Hair thinning. Science-fair exhibit: T-1 day.

W's bedroom blinds are closed, barring out the spring light. It isn't kind, this light. Lately it makes her skin sore.

Can you get up? I ask W at her bedside. I preferred it when she napped on the couch. There's less finality about a couch.

No answer. Daring to inch closer, closer than I can remember ever seeing her, I observe the pores on her forehead. Tiny craters. An unfamiliar landscape, the surface of the moon.

The eyelids shiver and I jump back. W opens her eyes, closes them, opens them again. Whoa, she says, her voice hoarse, as if she's waking from a lifelong sleep. She says, Here I thought you were the Lord Almighty himself, coming to visit me.

Not quite, I say. Can you get up?

W props herself up on one elbow, falls back, laughs. I get dizzy when I do this, she says.

It's just a few steps to the bathroom, I say.

You're taller, she says. How long have I been asleep? My God, you are giant. A thousand times taller than me.

I tell her to cut it out with the hallucinations, but she only laughs harder. Something hot starts climbing my spine and I count the blinds: 25. A perfect 25.

I'm still smaller than W, carrying her to the bathroom will be near impossible. I can't bring the scale to her—the carpeting on the bedroom floor will throw off the calibration. There's no way around it, I need that last little number.

I say, Put your arms around me, I can help you.

She's quiet now, as if there's magic to my words. Slowly, very slowly, her mouth stretches into a smile. She says, Okay. Okay.

I lean into her. She wraps one arm around me, then the other, and I start lifting her to a sitting position. I'm too fast at first. Maybe it's nerves or one of those brain glitches, when you grab a milk carton off the counter, thinking it'll be full and heavy, and you jerk it up because it turns out to be light. W feels so light. I imagine her bones hollowing. There's a smell to her, damp and sour, and I have trouble taking a full breath.

We hobble over to the bathroom, her limpness draped over me. Would you look at us, isn't this just the funniest, she says, I'm like a monkey on your back.

She steps on the scale, says I really do worry too much, and would I like to hear a song? For her full weight to register I tell her to let go of me for a second. She sings into my hair. *Wee Willie Winkie runs through the town.* She wants to kiss me on the nose, misses, jabs my eye. *Upstairs and downstairs in his nightgown.* She unwraps her arms and teeters on the spot. *Tapping at the window, crying at the lock.* I tell her her toes are covering the dial. *Are the children in their bed?* She shuffles her feet back. *Hey Willie Winkie see there he comes.* The dial twitches, stops. 105 pounds.

My arms and legs feel strange, as if they're the wrong size, a bad fit. Someone must have glued them onto me because they aren't mine. This body isn't mine. This house isn't mine. This isn't me.

Nifty Finds, photo department. Beach balls on the walls, happy babies happy people happy cats preserved in gloss, matte, semi-sheen finishes. Glass frames keep the fingers out. The girl stands at the counter, also glass, contemplating her own floating fingerprints, smearing them on the counter, the awful child. When future Lisa Ferrell (orange uniform, orange curls tied up) hands over the package of photos, does she give the girl a look? Hasn't she peeked inside the package? The girl shakes her head clean and it's a man behind the counter and he does not look at her at all.

I turn a page in my school planner and it asks me what my dream is, with fillable bullet points to achieve it. This is my dream: one day I will fly over to Mr. Brown, P.O. Box 450, Miami, FL, and his arm will envelop me like it enveloped W once in a photo I found slipped between the wall and dresser. On the back of the photo: *Wait for me and I'll take you someplace perfect.* I wonder if God promised W the same.

Edison school, gymnasium. The exhibits are covered in tablecloths, linens, blankets, ready for the unveiling. The girl enters. Her steps are even. She has decided against the swamp-green blouse with the buttons and front pocket. Her poster board, covered in black plastic, keeps slipping from her sweaty fingers. Under the covering: photos of W, diagrams, tallies and numbers, samples of the thin and thinning (hair, nails, other).

Klaus hops between exhibits, beaming at everyone. He helps Lisa Ferrell set up a tray of plants and a container with live flies for a demonstration. When Klaus sees the girl, he waves her over. He helps take the covering off her project, expecting to see Patches the martyr.

Klaus blinks once, twice. The third blink takes a good while to come.

What is this? he asks, stepping back, as if something about the poster or the girl is contagious. Klaus has it wrong. This is not how a person is supposed to act when they spot a winner.

It's a study of a human feeding on light, the girl answers, her voice softer than intended. And that's Subject Winifred.

Who's Subject Winifred? asks Klaus.

Silence.

Who is Subject Winifred? he repeats. Ricky Fielder and a few others start to make their way over. Klaus's hands shake as he covers the project back up. You'll need to come with me, he says.

Labyrinth of offices. A corner of the poster board is uncovered. Covered again. My dear. My dear, my dear. My . . . your name? When did . . . ? Why did she . . . ? Who can we . . . ? Isn't there someone we can . . . ? My dear. Stay here while we take a moment to . . .

Crouching in the closet, holding my flashlight to these pages. I did not submit the report at the end even though they tried to take it from me, Klaus. I'm not finished yet. I bet you think I forgot about the refeeding phase again. My ears prick up every time car tires crackle on the gravel outside. In the offices they asked me to confirm my address I don't remember what I said. They had fresh flowers in clean vases can't think of that now must finish this before they come.

In the next room lies W her body a crumple of sheets her hand cold. A minute ago the girl lay next to her humming touching the strangeness of that hand waiting for it to fuse into hers talking to it brushing the fingers over her face and the girl's shoes were still on she hadn't kicked them off when she burst into the house ran away from school.

Klaus, you asked the girl, Who is Subject Winifred?

She isn't my mother, Winnie, just like the girl isn't me. They must belong to a different exhibit, with a different outcome.

I'll tell you what happens to Winnie. I like this version better, and hope you can believe in it with me.

In the next room Winnie wakes. She stretches. She searches the kitchen cupboards, ready to eat her own tongue. I offer her some mango syrup and we have a rosy time, just like this, spooning syrup into each other's mouths, our cheeks sticky. Between spoonfuls she asks how I am and I ask how God is and she asks, God who? and our days stretch out like this, merrily merrily, one after the other until the closet door can't hold any more tallies.

DARLENE NAPONSE

SHE IS WATER

The River ran along the border of the reserve and the township. It was once a popular area to paddle down. Freshwater trout swam the river. In 1957, the plywood plant on the north shore of Lake Dark started production, dumping liquid garbage, from employees' shit and piss to formaldehyde, into the lake. Chemicals humans can't even pronounce were pushed, pumped, and forgotten. Thirty-five years later, an implausible number of puked-out litres of toxic waste in Lake Dark, the company closed its doors, yet it never cleaned up a drop of their hate. Lake Dark's natural outflow is The River.

⁓

Edna Redfoot once found a two-headed trout, or so she says at every band meeting, when she was fishing in the Lake. Robert Hurf once found a pickerel infested with vile, open sores. I believe that story 'cause I saw it in his garage. The pickerel had few scales left. As I stared at the sores, I felt them mutating, like alien heads rising from the circular, oozing tombs.

Every now and then, people sank cars, skidoos, bikes, washing machines, old love letters, boats, ashes, cans of Spam, cups, canoes, pants, panties, dresses, shoes, cowboy boots, fishing rods, beer bottles, cigarette butts, pop cans, and bodies in Lake Dark, the deepest lake in the region.

Kids swam at the beach in a roped-off area. The water was so turbulent and deep; I imagine it never has time to warm up. The last August swim is the most important. It is the one day you float on your back and watch the horizon disappear. You spend the day soaking in the sun and the water. You and your friends stay late at the beach. Once the sun falls behind the cedars, you know it is fall. The cool breeze makes the water unbearable to swim in after that day.

⚬⚬⚬

In the winter of 1989, two boys from town were crossing frozen Lake Dark. It was a warm winter, and many of the lakes in the area hadn't frozen over. The boys were heading home from a party and instead of driving around the lake, they decided to drive across. Their bodies and truck were never found. All that remained was their tracks and one eyewitness who saw them crossing about six in the morning. I imagined they found a better place to live, away from this small town.

My grandmother told me eight canoers died on Lake Dark in 1954. They went in the water too early. Spring is a bitch sometimes. The winds shifted them into the water.

Bodies began to be discovered, south of Lake Dark, in The River. Suzy Highground was found face up, naked, stuck in Tom Hunt's dock. She was twelve and from the reserve. The police never investigated; they said it was a swimming accident. Suzy won every swim contest on the reserve. She was walking home from school, twenty-one kilometres away from The River when she disappeared.

Annie TwoToes never had time to tell her story. She was found upriver by the Mayor's farm. No one ever heard what happened to her. Her parents closed their eyes and were never seen again.

⬯

When I was in school, I learned that rivers, creeks, and streams are tributaries. The word sounds like it should be known as greatness. These tributaries, the branches of Lake Dark, all had greatness.

The creek that ran north had the best trout run around. Me and my dad once pulled a fifteen-pound trout from that creek; my family ate trout for four days.

West of Lake Dark was a small stream that had this distant way of being. It was hard to walk along and full of rocks and deadfall. My older brother James once found a bear cub stuck in the rocks. He watched him for fifteen minutes and waited for the cub's mother to come back. As he was going to move the rocks, the mother bear returned. She walked around the cub, then started to dig. My brother hid behind a boulder. The mother bear growled, which my dad later told us was a moan of fear as it ripped apart the rocks. The mother bear and her cub ran away. James ran home to tell us his tale.

The western stream was the one area most townies never went. In the spring me and my cousins pick fiddleheads along the shoreline. My aunt June Feather would buy them for five cents a fiddlehead. She'd make a stew from them or fry them up. I never tried them. Aunt June said fiddleheads are the most wonderful thing in the world. I always thought Saturdays with my mom and brothers were the most wonderful thing in the world.

In the south is a small river and rapids. We liked to camp there. The water runs constantly, and my mom says, "It's the best place to catch whitefish." She told me the water is the cleanest in the area, because the water is always moving. I was confused till one hot day I watched the water in Lake Dark, and it never moved. I'm sure it did, but as the sweat dropped off my forehead into the water, the ripple was the only movement I saw.

We always gathered, fished, hunted, and lived near water when I was young. In the summer, we were never at our house. We often set camp out on The River for weeks. We ate fish and swam the whole summer. All my cousins would either stay with us, or their parents would set up camp. At night we played kick the can and hid in the hardwood bush. When the person who was IT finished counting to twenty by the can, they would go around looking for everyone and when they saw you they would run back to the can and say, "I see Julia." Then Julia would be out. If you were not good at finding people or not a fast runner, your cousin would come running out of the bush and kick the can, then you would be IT again. The older cousins always cheated and teamed up against us young ones. Then we teamed up and 'cause we were faster, we managed to be the ones hiding, not looking for everyone.

I asked my grandpa about The River. He said his mother was born across The River downstream. We lived where the water changed direction. In school, it is referred to as the area that separates the Atlantic and Arctic watersheds. They say the water starts to run north from this point.

He told me about the natural borders, the divides, and the height of land. He told me stories about the settlers divvying up land using the natural divides. I wondered how they could do that if the land wasn't theirs to give away?

❦

In the east, I was left to sleep. The water was deep. No one liked being around that part of The River. It always seems to take more away than you imagined.

❦

My grandpa lived on The River. He had a small farm that ran two kilometres along The River's bend. The bend is where all the fun starts. After the bend, the rapids begin. It's not like the Colorado River, but it was our rapids. When you paddled down it, you often lost a paddle or put a good dent or hole in your canoe.

When I was eleven, I tried taking an inflatable tube down The River. My cousins, my younger brother Davis, and I were pumped. Cousin Jack hit the jagged rocks in the front part of the rapids and never made it down; my other cousin Gent watched on the shoreline; Davis rode the tube like a knee board. He was fearless. Then right after the last calm, he dove into the water and knocked himself out on a boulder. I swam to get him. He was a big boy, always was. When he was born, he looked like a four-month baby boy. By age two, he stood taller than any of his cousins.

He floated to the surface face down. Jack ran to get my grandpa. I tried flipping him over. Gent jumped in and helped me drag him to the shore. We turned him over. Davis didn't breathe. Gent ran home. I kept screaming at Davis, hitting his chest, moving him sideways. I breathed into his mouth. I looked inside his mouth and asked the fish, the ants, the eagle, the crow to help him breathe but they all disappeared.

My grandpa sold his farm after Davis died. He moved us closer to the village, on the flattest, driest land, away from The River. My mother didn't say a word to me for seven days.

Weeks and months after Davis died, I wondered why the fish, the ants, the eagle, the crow all went away? They were always with me, aside from that evil salamander, who always seemed to escape my sight. The fish, the ants, the eagle, the crow watched over me.

———— ∞ ————

The truck came from behind me. I was trying to remember the words to "We Got the Beat" when he grabbed me. I was walking into town to meet up with my study group. I never saw him, nor did I know him. His large rough hands smelled of old ashtrays and gasoline.

When he put his hands over my mouth, I gagged and started to get sick. He pulled my arms and tied them behind my back. I was screaming. No one was around to hear. He tied a cloth over my eyes and pushed me into his truck. I threw up all over the truck and he punched me in the face.

By the time I started to breathe we were driving away. My stomach convulsed as he was shouting at me. Death metal rang and phased out his voice.

"'Jumpin' get down we got the beat. Round and round and round, We got the beat,'" I repeated over and over.

⸎

The River ran through the reserve, with its many creeks and streams running into it. We always seemed to be running south, following the creek. The reserve was a small area, a few houses, a band office, and a clinic. The clinic was in a rundown portable. We were all shipped out every morning on the yellow bus into town to go to school. School was fun for me. I liked all the classes. I never really liked the teachers; they were mean, but I liked the books. Science class was always interesting.

I imagined myself being an astronaut. I wanted to search the sky for intelligent life. I wanted to explore, like Captain Janeway, Commander of the Starfleet starship USS *Voyager.* I wanted to float in space, and walk on another planet. My mother bought me books on space.

We lived with my grandpa for a few years and my mother was making decent money at the truck stop. All the truckers liked it when she talked back. My mother had the worst potty mouth. She swore just like them. The truck stop was the perfect place to make tips. The men loved her comic rudeness and rewarded her for her antics.

When she came home she was exhausted. She would come in and kiss me goodnight. My mother wasn't that great with money so she gave me her tips and told me to hide them till Christmas or for school clothes for me and my brother.

I hid the money in a space book. The one space book I never really liked because its pictures were childish. I cut out an area and stashed the loonies, toonies, and five-dollar bills in the book. It filled quickly, so I cut up the encyclopedias we had. I was the only one who read in the house. My brother or my grandpa would never look in the books.

My grandpa had satellite. There were so many channels it was ridiculous. You could watch old films, new films, channels just for sports, channels just for music, channels in Spanish, and lots of commercials.

Each week we watched *Star Trek: Voyager.* My grandpa sat in his La-Z-Boy and I lay on the floor. I could smell the maple wood burning and the heat was constant. I didn't need a blanket or a pillow. During the commercial, I heard the cast-iron lever creak open; Grandpa was putting more wood in the fireplace. I loved watching the red-hot embers roll around. It was hypnotizing. Grandpa was slow putting the wood in and I always got extra seconds to see the embers turn to flame.

We watched as Captain Janeway and her crew travelled through space, moving past every obstacle challenging them. Would they make it home? They were diplomatic, saved lives, and kept to the Starfleet's ethical code of conduct. I wanted to work on a spaceship like the Captain. She kicked ass. She also sounded like she smoked a hundred Export As a day. Captain Janeway had a thing with Chakotay, the hunky Native American who was her First Officer. It was the first time I saw a native character who didn't have a loincloth and speak like a stoic illiterate on TV. I loved satellite TV.

Everything was aligning for me. I felt like I was a planet in the solar system.

———⊗⊗⊗———

My first kiss was under a full moon. I stood still waiting for something to happen in my body, a sign he was the one. He drove a dirt bike and sang with the Eagle Claw drum group. His hair was longer than mine. His lips were small and so soft, I wanted to plump them like a goose. We dated for a bit and had more fun running around in the bush than making out. We broke up and I decided to search only for boys with luscious lips and strong hands. It was a tall order, but I knew there was someone out there.

Davis always teased me about boys and said I would marry an ugly man with no teeth and have ten babies. I knew I was going to marry the hottest Indian at the Pow Wow and may not have any babies.

———⊗⊗⊗———

Our mother worked three jobs. She worked at the truck stop, was a part-time librarian, and sometimes she sold Tupperware. After Davis died, I went to work with her and didn't go to school for six months. She told the teachers she was home-schooling me. The school fought with my mother and said she didn't have the skills to home-school me. She said to test me when I returned and then if I was not up to their standards, I would lose my year.

The months after Davis died were strange. I liked being with my mom but when we had moments of fun, we stopped quickly, and started to do a chore. We both kinda looked at each other, then turned around and went our separate ways. I often found her outside in the yard looking west.

My older brother James was in his last year of high school and worked in a garage. We only saw him at breakfast or when he was home for dinner because he was broke. He never spoke of Davis nor of our father, who had disappeared one night on the reserve when I was seven. It was better our father had left; he wasn't that nice to our mother. He was an asshole from the drink.

I helped my mother at the truck stop in the mornings, then I read all afternoon while she worked at the library. She ordered so many books about space and aliens that year, the librarian had created a special section titled The Universe, The Cosmos, and Extraterrestrials. The magazines were the most popular thing for people to read at the library, and the librarian put the space collection, with a huge globe and planets hanging from the ceiling, right beside the magazines. It was the best place in the world.

Lake Dark recognized my obsession with space and aliens. I was walking to my friend's house. It was a cold December night and I was not dressed properly. I cut through old man Bob's farm and walked along the shoreline. I kept hearing this noise. It felt like it was under me. At first, I thought I was on the frozen lake. I stopped and looked for some ailing cow. Nothing was around me but the cold. The cows were in the barn. I was still along the farmland.

I listened in the darkness. I understood that under the water, aliens were speaking to me. No, I was not high; I never did that stuff. I was only twelve. Drones and murmurs echoed through my brain. The curved rhythms whirled and rose. It was a code. No, it was an unwritten message to me. Yes, it was the air escaping and the ice forming, but maybe it was from Davis or an alien calling out to me to play them a Pow Wow song. After an hour, I understood it. The water was speaking to me. I had to dream.

I returned to school in the winter and left at lunch and spent afternoons at the library.

They tried to expel me, but my mom dared them to test me. I passed every test, with high marks. The principal was so upset he walked out of the room.

My mom laughed and we ran out of the school straight to the car. On the way home, she bought a bucket of fried chicken for dinner. It was a celebration. We never had takeout; the only time we had fried chicken was at feasts and birthdays.

James came home that evening and after the greasy bucket of chicken, we told funny stories from the past. James finally told a story about Davis and hunting. In the middle he cried. It was the first time I saw him cry. Mom and I watched him cry. Then he looked up, said he missed Davis. It was the first time we all cried together.

Davis was the emptiness we all carried; he was the love we all understood. James finished his story. We laughed so much my mom fell off her chair.

———⟨∞∞⟩———

A month later, four owls sat outside my mother's door. She never saw more than two beside each other. The owls only came to her door when people she loved died.

She ran out the door and followed the owls down to The River.

———⟨∞∞⟩———

When the large man dumped me in the water, he held me under. The weeds rubbed against my bare legs. The River was cold; he broke the ice when he dropped me in The River. The pickerel came and sang an ancient song.

The tiny molecules of bacteria perfectly arranged themselves on my body, holding together all my skin.

My eyes were open and I saw everything. His face was filled with hate. His hands were still dirty. His hair was light brown and greasy.

It was Saturday, the spring of '97.

After he left, ice covered The River. A muskrat swam to me and closed my eyes with his tiny feet.

———⟨∞∞⟩———

I asked the fish, the ants, the eagle, the crow, and Davis to help me breathe. They floated with me. We were on the starship USS *Voyager* travelling a million light-years away.

LISA ALWARD

OLD GROWTH

Ray's realtor appears to have nothing on from the waist up. She flashes across the front window of her bungalow as if startled to see them drive into the yard, though Ray did text her from the ferry. Gwyneth glimpses shapely arms, a firm curve of breast.

"Your realtor's topless."

Ray leers across the steering wheel. "Whaaa?"

But it's just a nude T-shirt. Gwyneth can see this plainly now that the realtor has stepped outside in her sock feet and is smiling at them, or rather at Ray. A tall woman in her forties, reasonably slim with bushy blond hair, the top piece pulled back in a faded green scrunchy. No doubt the younger and more attractive of the two agents on the island: Ray would have done his research. Gwyneth would like to make another crack about this but feels too chastened by the T-shirt.

Anyway, she's too late. Ray has swung open the driver's door and is loping across the grass to give his realtor one of the bear hugs he reserves for small children and pretty women. Gwyneth pushes her own door ajar and extends one sandalled foot, inspecting her toenails in the late morning light. Purple, at her age, really? As she stands and unkinks her shoulders, Ray gives the blond woman a quick kiss near the mouth. Now, the two of them glance over. This could be interesting. Is he going to introduce her as his ex-wife? Or as his friend, his adviser, his financier? Of course, he might just say she's a hitchhiker. This was how he introduced her to his parents all those years ago, and Gwyneth, twenty-four and in love, played along the whole weekend, though they'd actually met tree planting and Ray had gone to the bus station to get her.

"Fern," Ray says, "Gwyneth. Gwyneth, Fern."

Fern smiles limply. Then, brightening, she says to Ray, "Just give me a sec," and turns back to the bungalow where a pair of hiking boots waits beside a painted chair.

She has a breathy little-girl voice, though on scrutiny looks closer to forty-nine than forty. Gwyneth tries to catch Ray's eye, but he is gazing around his realtor's property—three acres with a vegetable garden, an orchard, and a pen for her horses (Fern gives riding lessons on the side). Gwyneth knows his air of distraction is deliberate, that he's already pulling away from their tenuous connection on the drive up the coast. If she speaks now, he won't hear her, so intent will he be on communing with his realtor. Fern certainly seems flattered, pointing out the different types of apple trees and detailing the contents of the compost heap next to Ray's mud-splattered Focus.

Already, Gwyneth is regretting she's come.

I think I've found it, he'd announced on the phone. My land. And when she'd said, That's great, Ray, he surprised her by suggesting she drive to the island with him before he made his offer. They could get there and back in a day, and if they missed the last ferry, well, they could sleep in the car, like old times. Classic Ray. Yet he seemed so eager. C'mon, Gwyn. You can tell me if I'm crazy or not. And when she still hung back, I promise I'll be on my best behaviour. Neither of them mentioned the loan, but that's another reason he would want her to see it, so that she'll feel easier giving him the $20,000, and on the phone, perversely, this touched her. Not that she cares which piece of wilderness he buys. She's already made up her mind to loan him the money—for Cam and Jenna, so he'll have something to leave them, especially now that the cottage has finally sold and Ray is tearing through his share. It's your money, Ben had shrugged, but you know what he's like. As for doing a road trip with her ex-husband, he merely rolled his eyes. Maybe you can talk him out of it.

Ray at least was on time for once, early in fact. He had appeared preoccupied with a map while she was kissing Ben goodbye on the porch but smirked as she slid in beside him, Honeymoon still not over, I see. Then he buzzed down the driver's window and called out, Don't worry, man. I'll take good care of her. See you in two weeks! So that she had to reach across his skinny lap and shout, Tonight, Ben! See you tonight! As she eased back, she remarked, Still the same old asshole, I see, and Ray gave her a mock salute. But it seemed to relax them both, this allusion to a sexual rivalry that had never really existed—Ray being with Angie still when Gwyneth met Ben.

Still, it felt strange sharing a car with him again. He'd started combing his hair back, she noticed, no doubt to camouflage his bald spot, and the light green hemp shirt he was wearing— short-sleeved with a collar and looking like it could use a little ironing—was one she'd bought a couple of months ago for Cam to give him on Father's Day. In the store, she'd spent a long time fingering it, the fabric stiff like linen but with a hint of softness. So Ray. On the way out of the city, he detoured through a Tim's for coffees, and Gwyneth pulled back his tab and dabbed his jeans with their stack of napkins after he spilled the first sip. When Jenna texted, How's your holiday with Dad? Killed him yet? Gwyneth sent back a smiley face, Not yet. However, it was surprisingly relaxed, like catching up with an old friend. They talked about the kids (how great it was that Cam was finally getting his act together, and who was this new guy of Jenna's anyway?) and also about Ben. (He's a good man, Ray said. Solid. You deserve that, Gwyn.) They even joked about a few of his more harmless flaws—how she still has to remind him about his mother's birthday and the time he drove six hours to his brother's wedding without his suit. Mostly, though, they talked about the land.

The seller, a middle-aged German, would be leaving behind a half-built house, and Ray was debating whether he should finish it or use the lumber for his own cabin in the woods. Why didn't the German finish his house? Gwyneth asked. No idea, Ray grinned. Maybe he got bored, or his marriage fell apart. He had spent much of his summer Googling solar panels, composting toilets, organic gardening. A couple of pals were willing to help him build next year. In the meantime, he was hoping to find someone local (his realtor had a few names) to do the extra clearing he wanted. Then he would be able to quit his job and retire to the island, go off the grid. He looked at her with that intense light gaze, daring her to tear down this new plan. But that was one of the dispensations of being divorced so long: she would not criticize, not any-more. Sounds great, she said. Then thought of the vw bus he'd bought for $500 and left to rust in their driveway, the tree house he was always going to build for the kids, all those rot-ting boards behind the shed. You're going to love it, Ray enthused, tapping the steering wheel. Wait till you see all the old growth.

Fern won't stop going on about the trees either.

"Wait until you see the old-growth firs on Ray's land," she says, catching Gwyneth's eye in the rear-view mirror, as if signalling her to gush as well.

They have switched to the realtor's Outback and Gwyneth is already feeling carsick. Not only is she stuck in the back seat, but Fern keeps taking her hands off the wheel to talk, then jerking the wheel back in place to round another bend. Gwyneth wonders if calling the land Ray's before he's put in an offer is an old real estate trick. Even Ray is doing it now, worrying out loud that the farmer next door to his land might be tapping his maples.

When they first set out from the bungalow, she made a point of asking Fern about herself. The realtor explained that she had been born on the island, as were both her grannies, but that her parents left for the mainland in their teens, only to return with the back-to-the-land movement in the mid-'70s. Up until Fern was eight, they lived on a communal farm with two other families. She was home-schooled, but mostly she ran wild in the woods. Ray would like that, Gwyneth reflected. He'd always considered himself a latter-day hippie and often seemed dazed by their mortgage, the kids, his job teaching communications to blasé college students. Fern got along beautifully with the other realtor on the island (who made pottery on the side), and, no, she didn't know why the German had abandoned his house. When Gwyneth asked about her horses, she boasted that she'd been riding since she was three. That's a long time, Gwyneth said, but Fern laughed, I'm not that old. She kept waiting for Fern to ask a question back. Surely, she must wonder why Ray brought along this definitely old-already woman with the purple toenails. But Fern seemed no more curious about her than the dusty ostrich ferns lining the ditches.

Gwyneth directs a question now at Ray. "Have you looked into the water supply?"

"Oh, he doesn't need to be concerned about that," Fern says. "There's good access to groundwater everywhere on the island."

"Her partner's a civil engineer," Ray remarks, though he knows full well Ben is a tax lawyer.

"Are you okay?" Fern says into the mirror.

"I'm fine. I just get carsick in the back."

"Well, make sure you tell us if there's anything we can do to make you feel better," she says cheerily, turning to chat to Ray about his new neighbourhood while Ray surveys the dense bush with childlike wonder.

When she finally pulls over, asserting with an excited flick of the hand, "Here we are!" there is nothing to suggest they are anywhere, certainly no For Sale sign. Fern, however, hops out of the Outback and points to a stick smeared with pink paint on the side of the highway.

"The western marker for your property line, Ray."

Next, she unfurls a survey map that shows how the eight

acres begin narrow, then widen near the house before narrowing again for four more acres. Ray, of course, has seen the land before—clearly, this is how he's become so cozy with his realtor—but he frowns at the map and stares vaguely at Fern, as though he's forgotten who she is or why he's here. Gwyneth, who's seen him like this before, guesses he's starting to feel nervous about the prospect of going off-grid for real. Commitment has never been Ray's forte.

Fern doesn't seem to notice and leaps into the ditch. As Ray plunges in after her, he throws Gwyneth a quick backward grimace. "You coming?"

"You bet!"

On the phone, she did think to ask about footwear. Would sandals be okay? Yes, yes, he'd assured her. The German had dug a road in from the highway. But Fern must have decided to take an off-road route.

"You okay?" she calls back over her shoulder.

Huge rubbery leaves slap Gwyneth on the face. Bark grit jams beneath her toes. "Just fine."

Up ahead, Ray, who has regained his composure, is tilting his head close to his realtor's as she regales him about the natural attributes of his land. In addition to being a real estate agent and riding instructor, Fern appears to have an exhaustive knowledge of island flora and fauna. She is practically running now, showing off this big-leaf maple and that rare forest flower, noting how interesting it is that a cedar has rooted itself around the stump of a fir. She is quite the nature girl. No doubt, she also leads a Brownie troop on the side. Ray, however, Gwyneth observes with grumpy satisfaction, is even balder than she'd thought.

"Look at this, Ray."

Fern has stopped beside an enormous fallen tree. Someone has chain-sawed it into chunks, the largest spanning almost four feet. She nudges Ray's elbow, beckons Gwyneth.

"See the rings," she says, pointing at the largest chunk. "You can tell how old it is by counting them." Definitely a Brownie troop.

Now, she is caressing the outer rings with her fingertips, and Gwyneth worries that she might actually count them. Instead, she steps back, her yellow hair grazing Ray's hemp shirt.

"The rings look pretty much the same until you get right up close. Then you can see that some are wider, meaning an easy winter and long growing season, and some thinner, usually a hard winter and shorter growing season."

"Just like relationships," Ray quips, "except the best ones are usually the shortest."

Even Ray seems puzzled by what he's just said. He and Fern are still hovering by the rings, so Gwyneth rests her back against one of the smaller chunks of sawed tree and flaps her cardigan at the mosquitoes. She's promised herself that she won't think about Angie anymore. But the rings remind her. Once, she watched Ray and Angie standing together like this at a family bonfire—not talking or touching, just standing, and yet the force of their attraction cutting her to pieces. You know he's not monogamous? his own brother had warned her. She knew but married him anyway. What was she thinking? That the two of them were rooted together in some elemental way? That once he had a family he wouldn't stray? Watching Fern try to make sense of his joke about the rings, Gwyneth almost feels sorry for her. It's Ray who turns her into such a bitch—even now when there's nothing between them but their almost-grown children and this loan. Why should she care anymore who he screws around with? She is supposed to be done with all that, starting over fresh with Ben.

But he still gets to her. She should have known this. She did know. All the time they were talking in the car, on the phone as well, she'd been softening, feeling the nearness of the old Ray—the one who kissed her breasts before babies, who was always floating off somewhere but still could somehow make her laugh. Even the wrinkled hemp shirt is a tendril, pulling her back. But she'd been a fool to think he wore it for her.

She heaves herself forward. "Are we anywhere near the road yet?"

"It's just ahead," Fern sings out.

The road is nothing but a grassy track and the house, when it materializes, weirdly narrow with a tin roof that juts so far out that the two storeys look in danger of tipping over. Beside it sits a leaf-strewn camper van and, in front, a rusted pickup truck. The scene has a haphazard sleepiness about it, as if the German has merely gone out for supplies and forgotten to come back.

Now that they have reached their destination, Ray seems about to break into a jig. "What do you think?"

"What's with the roof?"

"We think he must have been planning to build two screened-in porches, one on top of the other," Fern says. "That's why the roof's so extended."

"Is that the only door?' Gwyneth points at a large triangular opening on the second floor.

"Oh, no," Fern laughs. "We think that was meant to be the entrance to the upper porch. The door's around the side."

Ray and Fern stride ahead, murmuring back and forth, while Gwyneth picks her way through the nails and shards of wood that litter the long grass. She has wrapped her cardigan around her face to keep away the bugs and knows without looking that the purple polish is all chipped now.

Inside the house, Ray is suddenly attentive again, showing her a table of good-quality tools the German has left behind and cautioning her, as they climb the rough stairs to the second floor, to stick to the crossbeams and not stand too close to that triangular hole in the wall. He is especially proud of a curious window that shutters from the inside and can be opened only by pulling across a wooden dowel. This dowel is about a foot long and carved with leaves and flowers. It is the one detail of the house that is truly finished.

"It's beautiful, isn't it?" Fern whispers, fingering a petal, and Ray looks anxiously at Gwyneth.

This appeal is so hapless that she can't at first respond. Instead, she glances over the edge of the gaping triangle, which in that moment seems a perfect metaphor for their unfinished marriage. Large flakes of brown paint are starting to drift loose from the cab of the German's truck. Nearby, a plastic tarp clings by blue threads to a pile of mossy lumber. The tarp looks like Ray's faded one-man tent from their tree-planting summer. There's something you need to know, he told her that first night she shared it with him. He was older, had hitched to Mexico, was known around the camp for breaking hearts. I've always been a free spirit. I can't help it. I just blow with the wind. Tangled up inside his sleeping bag, with the shadows of the treetops moving above, she hadn't understood, or cared much, what this blowing might mean. She knew only that she wanted to curl herself around his body, so thin and pale in the tent light, and not let go. I think I'm in love with you, he also said, lifting her bangs. And she'd felt sure he meant it, because he looked so surprised.

Gwyneth sighs and faces him again. The German was clearly insane. She can't believe Ray is considering finishing the man's house. It will take him years, if he manages even to stick with it. Really, Ben was right. The idea of his going off-grid is ridiculous—what does Ray know about organic gardening? She watches him toss a screwdriver of the German's from one hand to the other, his pale blue eyes fixed on her, wanting her to say something nice about a dowel. What is she even doing here? He must know she lacks his realtor's breezy confidence that he can pull this off. And if he is concerned about the money, why risk her seeing the land, or for that matter seeing him with Fern? Then it all seems so obvious. He is as stuck as she is. Even now, he can't make a move without turning back to see if she will stop him. Some free spirit—more a tangled kite, twisting in the wind. And for the first time all day, she feels like laughing.

"Nice workmanship," she says at last, and when Fern asks what she thinks of the rest of the house, she smiles sweetly, "I think it has real potential."

Fern wants to take Ray to see the very end of the property. Gwyneth says she is still a little carsick and would rather wait. Against the side of the house, they find her a bench—just a narrow workbench pocked with ant holes, though she insists it's perfect. Both of them seem to want her permission to leave, Fern asking a couple more times if she's sure she'll be okay. But she smiles and waves them into wilderness. When she can't hear their voices, she lies back on the bench. Ray's trees are shifting overhead as though preparing to uproot themselves and walk away. Not that they can, any more than Ray. She pictures the two of them out on his land, the giant ferns gently stroking their bare arms, not talking so much now. Ray will be watching for a spot where the ground is soft, where he can pull her down. Or maybe Fern, impatient for his touch, will seize his hand and press him against an ancient maple. Let them do it. She wants them to. Let him add another ring. Even if they forget about her, desert her on this bench by the mad German's half-house, it will make no difference. The sun can go down, the air turn chill, the house cave in behind her. She will be here, waiting.

ABOUT THE CONTRIBUTORS

Lisa Alward was born in Halifax and lives in Fredericton. Her story "Old Growth" won *The New Quarterly*'s Peter Hinchcliffe Short Fiction Award in 2016 and has been selected for *The Best Canadian Stories 2017*. She won *The Fiddlehead* Short Fiction Prize in 2015 and was recently longlisted for *PRISM international*'s Jacob Zilber Prize for Short Fiction. Her work has appeared in *16: Best Canadian Stories* as well as *The Fiddlehead, The New Quarterly*, and *The Dalhousie Review*. She is completing a collection of stories.

Sharon Bala lives on a rock in the cold North Atlantic. In lieu of fan mail, please send mangoes. Her debut novel, *The Boat People*, will be on shelves January 2018. Sharon is a member of The Port Authority, a St. John's writing group. Her short stories have been published in *Hazlitt, Grain, PRISM international, The Dalhousie Review, The New Quarterly, Room, Riddle Fence*, and in a collection called *Racket: New Writing Made in Newfoundland*. Find her online at sharonbala.com.

Patrick Doerksen spent his childhood at the feet of British Columbia's mountains and his teen years on Saskatchewan's prairies. Now, after studying in Berlin, he is back in Vancouver. He publishes haiku, memorizes German compound words, and has recently graduated with a degree in social work. "Leech," which originally appeared in (*parenthetical*), is his first published story. He continues to publish short fiction and is at work on a novel.

Sarah Kabamba loves storytelling in all its forms, and believes that it is one of the most powerful tools given to artists. Her work has been published in *Carleton Now*, *Room*, and *In/Words Magazine & Press*. A recent graduate from Carleton University, she currently resides in Ottawa, where she is working on a collection of poetry.

Michael Meagher completed a Master of Arts in English and Creative Writing at the University of New Brunswick in 2015, where he received the David H. Walker Prize. His writing has appeared in journals such as *The Antigonish Review*, *The Fiddlehead*, *The Malahat Review*, and *PRISM international*. He is currently readying a collection of short stories for publication.

Darlene Naponse is an Anishinaabe from Atikameksheng Anishnawbek, Northern Ontario, where she was born and raised. She is a writer, independent film director, video artist, and community activist. She completed her MFA in Creative Writing at the Institute of American Indian Arts (IAIA) in Santa Fe. Several of her short stories have been published in the *Yellow Medicine Review*, *Along the 46th Anthology*, and *The Malahat Review*. She is currently working on a book of short stories. She works from her studio on the Rez (Atikameksheng Anishnawbek).

Maria Reva was born in Ukraine and grew up in Vancouver. Her stories have appeared, or are forthcoming, in *The Atlantic*, *The Malahat Review*, *The New Quarterly*, *The Guardian* (as part of *Tin House* Flash Fridays), and *The Best American Short Stories 2017*. Her musical collaborations include an opera libretto for ERATO Ensemble, texts for Vancouver International Song Institute's Art Song Lab, and a script for City Opera Vancouver. She is currently pursuing an MFA at the Michener Center for Writers (University of Texas at Austin), where she is at work on a linked story collection set in Soviet Ukraine.

Jack Wang holds an MFA in Creative Writing from the University of Arizona and a Ph.D. in English/Creative Writing from Florida State University. His fiction has appeared in *The Malahat Review*, *The New Quarterly*, *The Humber Literary Review*, and *Joyland*, and was shortlisted for the 2014 Commonwealth Short Story Prize. The recipient of the 2014–15 David T.K. Wong Creative Writing Fellowship from the University of East Anglia in England, he teaches writing at Ithaca College in upstate New York, where he is completing a collection of stories and a novella.

Kelly Ward is a Toronto-based writer and editor. She is the author of *Keep It Beautiful: Stories*, and winner of the Lush Triumphant Literary Award for Fiction. By day, she is managing editor of a small, independent publisher.

For more information about the publications that submitted to this year's competition, The Journey Prize, and *The Journey Prize Stories*, please visit www.facebook.com/TheJourneyPrize.

The Malahat Review is a quarterly journal of contemporary poetry, fiction, and creative non-fiction by both new and celebrated writers. Summer issues feature the winners of *Malahat*'s Novella and Long Poem prizes, held in alternate years; the fall issues feature the winners of the Far Horizons Award for emerging writers, alternating between poetry and fiction each year; the winter issues feature the winners of the Constance Rooke Creative Non-fiction Prize; and the spring issues feature winners of the Open Season Awards in all three genres (poetry, fiction, and creative non-fiction). All issues feature covers by noted Canadian visual artists and include reviews of Canadian books. Editor: John Barton. Assistant Editor: Rhonda Batchelor. Correspondence: *The Malahat Review*, University of Victoria, P.O. Box 1700, Station csc, Victoria, British Columbia, V8W 2Y2. Unsolicited submissions are accepted through Submittable only; contest entries, by email (review contest guidelines before entering). E-mail: malahat@uvic.ca Website: www.malahatreview.ca Twitter: @malahatreview

The New Quarterly is an award-winning literary magazine publishing fiction, poetry, personal essays, interviews, and essays on writing. Now in its thirty-sixth year, the magazine prides itself on its independent take on the Canadian literary scene. Recent issues include a Visual Storytelling Issue and our Fall 2016 celebration of diverse voices, with more exciting projects in the works. Editor: Pamela Mulloy. Submissions and correspondence: *The New Quarterly*, c/o St. Jerome's University, 290 Westmount Road North, Waterloo, Ontario, N2L 3G3. E-mail: pmulloy@tnq.ca, sblom@tnq.ca Website: www.tnq.ca

(parenthetical) is a hand-bound literary journal published bi-monthly by the micropress words(on)pages. For three years, *(parenthetical)* published poetry and fiction from some of the best new writers in Canada and beyond, from first-time publications to pieces from writers with a first book on the way. After twenty issues published online and in print, *(parenthetical)* is taking a brief hiatus, during which all content can be read online at wordsonpagespress.com/parenthetical. As such, *(parenthetical)* is not currently accepting submissions. Founding editors: Nicole Brewer and William Kemp. Correspondence: 216-120 Raglan Ave, Toronto, Ontario, M6C 2L4. Email: words@wordsonpagespress.com

PRISM international, the oldest literary magazine in Western Canada, was established in 1959 by Earle Birney at the University of British Columbia. Published four times a year, *PRISM* features short fiction, poetry, creative non-fiction, drama, and translations. *PRISM* editors select work based on originality and quality, and the magazine showcases work from both new and established writers from Canada and around the world. *PRISM* holds three exemplary annual competitions for short fiction, literary non-fiction, and poetry, and awards the Earle Birney Prize for Poetry to an outstanding poet whose work was featured in *PRISM* in the preceding year. Executive Editors: Selina Boan and Curtis LeBlanc. Prose Editor: Christopher Evans. Poetry Editor: Shaun Robinson. Reviews Editor: Anita Bedell. Submissions and correspondence: *PRISM international*, Creative Writing Program, The University of British Columbia, Buchanan E-462, 1866 Main Mall, Vancouver, British Columbia, V6T 1Z1. Website: www.prismmagazine.ca

Room magazine publishes fiction, poetry, creative non-fiction, and artwork by and about women. *Room* was founded in 1975 (as *Room of One's Own*) to provide opportunities for emerging and established writers and artists who identify as women to publish their work in Canada. Contributors have included some of Canada's most celebrated writers, including Alice Munro, Jane Urquhart, Larissa Lai, Carol Shields, Karen Solie, Pamela Porter, Elizabeth Bachinsky, and Betsy Warland. Each quarter we publish original, thought-provoking works that reflect women's strength, sensuality, vulnerability, and wit. Correspondence: *Room* magazine, Box 46160 Stn. D, Vancouver, British Columbia, V6J 5G5. Submissions: roommagazine.com/submit Website: roommagazine.com Email: contactus@roommagazine.com

Taddle Creek often is asked to define itself and, just as often, it tends to refuse to do so. But it will say this: each issue of the magazine contains a multitude of things between its snazzily illustrated covers, including, but not limited to, fiction, poetry, comics, art, interviews, and feature stories. It's an odd mix, to be sure, which is why *Taddle Creek* refers to itself somewhat oddly as a "general-interest literary magazine." Work presented in *Taddle Creek* is humorous, poignant, ephemeral, urban, and rarely overly earnest, though not usually all at once. *Taddle Creek* takes its mission to be the journal for those who detest everything the literary magazine has become in the twenty-first century very seriously. Editor-in-Chief: Conan Tobias. Correspondence: *Taddle Creek*, P.O. Box 611, Stn. P, Toronto, Ontario M5S 2Y4. E-mail: editor@taddlecreekmag.com. Website: taddlecreekmag.com.

Submissions were also received from the following publications:

Agnes and True
www.agnesandtrue.com

The Antigonish Review
(Antigonish, NS)
www.antigonishreview.com

Briarpatch Magazine
(Regina, SK)
www.briarpatchmagazine.com

Cosmonauts Avenue
(Montreal, QC)
www.cosmonautsavenue.com

Don't Talk to Me About Love
www.donttalktomeabout
love.org

EVENT
(New Westminster, BC)
www.eventmagazine.ca

The Fiddlehead
(Fredericton, BC)
www.TheFiddlehead.ca

Found Press
www.foundpress.com

FreeFall Magazine
(Calgary, AB)
www.freefallmagazine.ca

Glass Buffalo
(Edmonton, AB)
www.glassbuffalo.com

Humber Literary Review
www.humberliterary
review.com

The Impressment Gang
(Halifax, NS)
www.theimpressmentgang.com

Joyland Magazine
www.joylandmagazine.com

Little Fiction | Big Truths
(Toronto, ON)
www.littlefiction.com

Maisonneuve
(Montreal, QC)
www.maisonneuve.org

The New Orphic Review
(Nelson, BC)

Prairie Fire Press Inc.
(Winnipeg, MB)
www.prairiefire.ca

*The Prairie Journal of
Canadian Literature*
(Calgary, AB)
www.prairiejournal.org

PULP Literature
(Vancouver, BC)
www.pulpliterature.com

The Puritan
www.puritan-magazine.com

Ricepaper Magazine
(Vancouver, BC)
www.ricepapermagazine.ca

Riddle Fence
(St. John's, NL)
www.riddlefence.com)

The Rusty Toque
www.therustytoque.com

subTerrain Magazine
(Vancouver, BC)
www.subterrain.ca

This Magazine
(Toronto, ON)
www.this.org

The Walrus
(Toronto, ON)
www.thewalrus.ca

PREVIOUS CONTRIBUTING AUTHORS

* Winners of the $10,000 Journey Prize
** Co-winners of the $10,000 Journey Prize

1

1989
SELECTED WITH ALISTAIR MacLEOD

Ven Begamudré, "Word Games"
David Bergen, "Where You're From"
Lois Braun, "The Pumpkin-Eaters"
Constance Buchanan, "Man with Flying Genitals"
Ann Copeland, "Obedience"
Marion Douglas, "Flags"
Frances Itani, "An Evening in the Café"
Diane Keating, "The Crying Out"
Thomas King, "One Good Story, That One"
Holley Rubinsky, "Rapid Transits"*
Jean Rysstad, "Winter Baby"
Kevin Van Tighem, "Whoopers"
M.G. Vassanji, "In the Quiet of a Sunday Afternoon"
Bronwen Wallace, "Chicken 'N' Ribs"
Armin Wiebe, "Mouse Lake"
Budge Wilson, "Waiting"

2

1990
SELECTED WITH LEON ROOKE; GUY VANDERHAEGHE

André Alexis, "Despair: Five Stories of Ottawa"
Glen Allen, "The Hua Guofeng Memorial Warehouse"
Marusia Bociurkiw, "Mama, Donya"
Virgil Burnett, "Billfrith the Dreamer"
Margaret Dyment, "Sacred Trust"
Cynthia Flood, "My Father Took a Cake to France"*
Douglas Glover, "Story Carved in Stone"
Terry Griggs, "Man with the Axe"
Rick Hillis, "Limbo River"

Thomas King, "The Dog I Wish I Had, I Would Call It Helen"
K.D. Miller, "Sunrise Till Dark"
Jennifer Mitton, "Let Them Say"
Lawrence O'Toole, "Goin' to Town with Katie Ann"
Kenneth Radu, "A Change of Heart"
Jenifer Sutherland, "Table Talk"
Wayne Tefs, "Red Rock and After"

3
1991
SELECTED WITH JANE URQUHART

Donald Aker, "The Invitation"
Anton Baer, "Yukon"
Allan Barr, "A Visit from Lloyd"
David Bergen, "The Fall"
Rai Berzins, "Common Sense"
Diana Hartog, "Theories of Grief"
Diane Keating, "The Salem Letters"
Yann Martel, "The Facts Behind the Helsinki Roccamatios"*
Jennifer Mitton, "Polaroid"
Sheldon Oberman, "This Business with Elijah"
Lynn Podgurny, "Till Tomorrow, Maple Leaf Mills"
James Riseborough, "She Is Not His Mother"
Patricia Stone, "Living on the Lake"

4
1992
SELECTED WITH SANDRA BIRDSELL

David Bergen, "The Bottom of the Glass"
Maria A. Billion, "No Miracles Sweet Jesus"
Judith Cowan, "By the Big River"
Steven Heighton, "How Beautiful upon the Mountains"
Steven Heighton, "A Man Away from Home Has No Neighbours"
L. Rex Kay, "Travelling"
Rozena Maart, "No Rosa, No District Six"*
Guy Malet De Carteret, "Rainy Day"
Carmelita McGrath, "Silence"
Michael Mirolla, "A Theory of Discontinuous Existence"
Diane Juttner Perreault, "Bella's Story"
Eden Robinson, "Traplines"

5
1993
SELECTED WITH GUY VANDERHAEGHE

Caroline Adderson, "Oil and Dread"
David Bergen, "La Rue Prevette"
Marina Endicott, "With the Band"
Dayv James-French, "Cervine"
Michael Kenyon, "Durable Tumblers"
K.D. Miller, "A Litany in Time of Plague"
Robert Mullen, "Flotsam"
Gayla Reid, "Sister Doyle's Men"*
Oakland Ross, "Bang-bang"
Robert Sherrin, "Technical Battle for Trial Machine"
Carol Windley, "The Etruscans"

6
1994
SELECTED WITH DOUGLAS GLOVER;
JUDITH CHANT (CHAPTERS)

Anne Carson, "Water Margins: An Essay on Swimming by My Brother"
Richard Cumyn, "The Sound He Made"
Genni Gunn, "Versions"
Melissa Hardy, "Long Man the River"*
Robert Mullen, "Anomie"
Vivian Payne, "Free Falls"
Jim Reil, "Dry"
Robyn Sarah, "Accept My Story"
Joan Skogan, "Landfall"
Dorothy Speak, "Relatives in Florida"
Alison Wearing, "Notes from Under Water"

7

1995

SELECTED WITH M.G. VASSANJI;
RICHARD BACHMANN (A DIFFERENT DRUMMER BOOKS)

Michelle Alfano, "Opera"

Mary Borsky, "Maps of the Known World"

Gabriella Goliger, "Song of Ascent"

Elizabeth Hay, "Hand Games"

Shaena Lambert, "The Falling Woman"

Elise Levine, "Boy"

Roger Burford Mason, "The Rat-Catcher's Kiss"

Antanas Sileika, "Going Native"

Kathryn Woodward, "Of Marranos and Gilded Angels"*

8

1996

SELECTED WITH OLIVE SENIOR;
BEN MCNALLY (NICHOLAS HOARE LTD.)

Rick Bowers, "Dental Bytes"

David Elias, "How I Crossed Over"

Elyse Gasco, "Can You Wave Bye Bye, Baby?"*

Danuta Gleed, "Bones"

Elizabeth Hay, "The Friend"

Linda Holeman, "Turning the Worm"

Elaine Littman, "The Winner's Circle"

Murray Logan, "Steam"

Rick Maddocks, "Lessons from the Sputnik Diner"

K.D. Miller, "Egypt Land"

Gregor Robinson, "Monster Gaps"

Alma Subasic, "Dust"

9
1997
**SELECTED WITH NINO RICCI; NICHOLAS PASHLEY
(UNIVERSITY OF TORONTO BOOKSTORE)**

Brian Bartlett, "Thomas, Naked"

Dennis Bock, "Olympia"

Kristen den Hartog, "Wave"

Gabriella Goliger, "Maladies of the Inner Ear"**

Terry Griggs, "Momma Had a Baby"

Mark Anthony Jarman, "Righteous Speedboat"

Judith Kalman, "Not for Me a Crown of Thorns"

Andrew Mullins, "The World of Science"

Sasenarine Persaud, "Canada Geese and Apple Chatney"

Anne Simpson, "Dreaming Snow"**

Sarah Withrow, "Ollie"

Terence Young, "The Berlin Wall"

10
1998
**SELECTED BY PETER BUITENHUIS; HOLLEY RUBINSKY;
CELIA DUTHIE (DUTHIE BOOKS LTD.)**

John Brooke, "The Finer Points of Apples"*

Ian Colford, "The Reason for the Dream"

Libby Creelman, "Cruelty"

Michael Crummey, "Serendipity"

Stephen Guppy, "Downwind"

Jane Eaton Hamilton, "Graduation"

Elise Levine, "You Are You Because Your Little Dog Loves You"

Jean McNeil, "Bethlehem"

Liz Moore, "Eight-Day Clock"

Edward O'Connor, "The Beatrice of Victoria College"

Tim Rogers, "Scars and Other Presents"

Denise Ryan, "Marginals, Vivisections, and Dreams"

Madeleine Thien, "Simple Recipes"

Cheryl Tibbetts, "Flowers of Africville"

11
1999
SELECTED BY LESLEY CHOYCE; SHELDON CURRIE;
MARY-JO ANDERSON (FROG HOLLOW BOOKS)

Mike Barnes, "In Florida"

Libby Creelman, "Sunken Island"

Mike Finigan, "Passion Sunday"

Jane Eaton Hamilton, "Territory"

Mark Anthony Jarman, "Travels into Several Remote Nations of the World"

Barbara Lambert, "Where the Bodies Are Kept"

Linda Little, "The Still"

Larry Lynch, "The Sitter"

Sandra Sabatini, "The One With the News"

Sharon Steams, "Brothers"

Mary Walters, "Show Jumping"

Alissa York, "The Back of the Bear's Mouth"*

12
2000
SELECTED BY CATHERINE BUSH; HAL NIEDZVIECKI;
MARC GLASSMAN (PAGES BOOKS AND MAGAZINES)

Andrew Gray, "The Heart of the Land"

Lee Henderson, "Sheep Dub"

Jessica Johnson, "We Move Slowly"

John Lavery, "The Premier's New Pyjamas"

J.A. McCormack, "Hearsay"

Nancy Richler, "Your Mouth Is Lovely"

Andrew Smith, "Sightseeing"

Karen Solie, "Onion Calendar"

Timothy Taylor, "Doves of Townsend"*

Timothy Taylor, "Pope's Own"

Timothy Taylor, "Silent Cruise"

R.M. Vaughan, "Swan Street"

13
2001
SELECTED BY ELYSE GASCO; MICHAEL HELM;
MICHAEL NICHOLSON (INDIGO BOOKS & MUSIC INC.)

Kevin Armstrong, "The Cane Field"*

Mike Barnes, "Karaoke Mon Amour"

Heather Birrell, "Machaya"

Heather Birrell, "The Present Perfect"

Craig Boyko, "The Gun"

Vivette J. Kady, "Anything That Wiggles"

Billie Livingston, "You're Taking All the Fun Out of It"

Annabel Lyon, "Fishes"

Lisa Moore, "The Way the Light Is"

Heather O'Neill, "Little Suitcase"

Susan Rendell, "In the Chambers of the Sea"

Tim Rogers, "Watch"

Margrith Schraner, "Dream Dig"

14
2002
SELECTED BY ANDRÉ ALEXIS;
DEREK MCCORMACK; DIANE SCHOEMPERLEN

Mike Barnes, "Cogagwee"

Geoffrey Brown, "Listen"

Jocelyn Brown, "Miss Canada"*

Emma Donoghue, "What Remains"

Jonathan Goldstein, "You Are a Spaceman With Your Head Under the Bathroom Stall Door"

Robert McGill, "Confidence Men"

Robert McGill, "The Stars Are Falling"

Nick Melling, "Philemon"

Robert Mullen, "Alex the God"

Karen Munro, "The Pool"

Leah Postman, "Being Famous"

Neil Smith, "Green Fluorescent Protein"

15

2003

SELECTED BY MICHELLE BERRY;
TIMOTHY TAYLOR; MICHAEL WINTER

Rosaria Campbell, "Reaching"

Hilary Dean, "The Lemon Stories"

Dawn Rae Downton, "Hansel and Gretel"

Anne Fleming, "Gay Dwarves of America"

Elyse Friedman, "Truth"

Charlotte Gill, "Hush"

Jessica Grant, "My Husband's Jump"*

Jacqueline Honnet, "Conversion Classes"

S.K. Johannesen, "Resurrection"

Avner Mandelman, "Cuckoo"

Tim Mitchell, "Night Finds Us"

Heather O'Neill, "The Difference Between Me and Goldstein"

16

2004

SELECTED BY ELIZABETH HAY; LISA MOORE; MICHAEL REDHILL

Anar Ali, "Baby Khaki's Wings"

Kenneth Bonert, "Packers and Movers"

Jennifer Clouter, "Benny and the Jets"

Daniel Griffin, "Mercedes Buyer's Guide"

Michael Kissinger, "Invest in the North"

Devin Krukoff, "The Last Spark"*

Elaine McCluskey, "The Watermelon Social"

William Metcalfe, "Nice Big Car, Rap Music Coming Out the Window"

Lesley Millard, "The Uses of the Neckerchief"

Adam Lewis Schroeder, "Burning the Cattle at Both Ends"

Michael V. Smith, "What We Wanted"

Neil Smith, "Isolettes"

Patricia Rose Young, "Up the Clyde on a Bike"

17
2005
SELECTED BY JAMES GRAINGER AND NANCY LEE

Randy Boyagoda, "Rice and Curry Yacht Club"
Krista Bridge, "A Matter of Firsts"
Josh Byer, "Rats, Homosex, Saunas, and Simon"
Craig Davidson, "Failure to Thrive"
McKinley M. Hellenes, "Brighter Thread"
Catherine Kidd, "Green-Eyed Beans"
Pasha Malla, "The Past Composed"
Edward O'Connor, "Heard Melodies Are Sweet"
Barbara Romanik, "Seven Ways into Chandigarh"
Sandra Sabatini, "The Dolphins at Sainte Marie"
Matt Shaw, "Matchbook for a Mother's Hair"*
Richard Simas, "Anthropologies"
Neil Smith, "Scrapbook"
Emily White, "Various Metals"

18
2006
SELECTED BY STEVEN GALLOWAY;
ZSUZSI GARTNER; ANNABEL LYON

Heather Birrell, "BriannaSusannaAlana"*
Craig Boyko, "The Baby"
Craig Boyko, "The Beloved Departed"
Nadia Bozak, "Heavy Metal Housekeeping"
Lee Henderson, "Conjugation"
Melanie Little, "Wrestling"
Matthew Rader, "The Lonesome Death of Joseph Fey"
Scott Randall, "Law School"
Sarah Selecky, "Throwing Cotton"
Damian Tarnopolsky, "Sleepy"
Martin West, "Cretacea"
David Whitton, "The Eclipse"
Clea Young, "Split"

19
2007
**SELECTED BY CAROLINE ADDERSON;
DAVID BEZMOZGIS; DIONNE BRAND**

Andrew J. Borkowski, "Twelve Versions of Lech"
Craig Boyko, "OZY"*
Grant Buday, "The Curve of the Earth"
Nicole Dixon, "High-Water Mark"
Krista Foss, "Swimming in Zanzibar"
Pasha Malla, "Respite"
Alice Petersen, "After Summer"
Patricia Robertson, "My Hungarian Sister"
Rebecca Rosenblum, "Chilly Girl"
Nicholas Ruddock, "How Eunice Got Her Baby"
Jean Van Loon, "Stardust"

20
2008
SELECTED BY LYNN COADY; HEATHER O'NEILL; NEIL SMITH

Théodora Armstrong, "Whale Stories"
Mike Christie, "Goodbye Porkpie Hat"
Anna Leventhal, "The Polar Bear at the Museum"
Naomi K. Lewis, "The Guiding Light"
Oscar Martens, "Breaking on the Wheel"
Dana Mills, "Steaming for Godthab"
Saleema Nawaz, "My Three Girls"*
Scott Randall, "The Gifted Class"
S. Kennedy Sobol, "Some Light Down"
Sarah Steinberg, "At Last at Sea"
Clea Young, "Chaperone"

21

2009

SELECTED BY CAMILLA GIBB;
LEE HENDERSON; REBECCA ROSENBLUM

Daniel Griffin, "The Last Great Works of Alvin Cale"

Jesus Hardwell, "Easy Living"

Paul Headrick, "Highlife"

Sarah Keevil, "Pyro"

Adrian Michael Kelly, "Lure"

Fran Kimmel, "Picturing God's Ocean"

Lynne Kutsukake, "Away"

Alexander MacLeod, "Miracle Mile"

Dave Margoshes, "The Wisdom of Solomon"

Shawn Syms, "On the Line"

Sarah L. Taggart, "Deaf"

Yasuko Thanh, "Floating Like the Dead"*

22

2010

SELECTED BY PASHA MALLA; JOAN THOMAS; ALISSA YORK

Carolyn Black, "Serial Love"

Andrew Boden, "Confluence of Spoors"

Laura Boudreau, "The Dead Dad Game"

Devon Code, "Uncle Oscar"*

Danielle Egan, "Publicity"

Krista Foss, "The Longitude of Okay"

Lynne Kutsukake, "Mating"

Ben Lof, "When in the Field with Her at His Back"

Andrew MacDonald, "Eat Fist!"

Eliza Robertson, "Ship's Log"

Mike Spry, "Five Pounds Short and Apologies to Nelson Algren"

Damian Tarnopolsky, "Laud We the Gods"

23
2011
SELECTED BY ALEXANDER MacLEOD;
ALISON PICK; SARAH SELECKY

Jay Brown, "The Girl from the War"   .
Michael Christie, "The Extra"
Seyward Goodhand, "The Fur Trader's Daughter"
Miranda Hill, "Petitions to Saint Chronic"*
Fran Kimmel, "Laundry Day"
Ross Klatte, "First-Calf Heifer"
Michelle Serwatuk, "My Eyes Are Dim"
Jessica Westhead, "What I Would Say"
Michelle Winters, "Toupée"
D.W. Wilson, "The Dead Roads"

24
2012
SELECTED BY MICHAEL CHRISTIE;
KATHRYN KUITENBROUWER; KATHLEEN WINTER

Kris Bertin, "Is Alive and Can Move"
Shashi Bhat, "Why I Read *Beowulf*"
Astrid Blodgett, "Ice Break"
Trevor Corkum, "You Were Loved"
Nancy Jo Cullen, "Ashes"
Kevin Hardcastle, "To Have to Wait"
Andrew Hood, "I'm Sorry and Thank You"
Andrew Hood, "Manning"
Grace O'Connell, "The Many Faces of Montgomery Clift"
Jasmina Odor, "Barcelona"
Alex Pugsley, "Crisis on Earth-X"*
Eliza Robertson, "Sea Drift"
Martin West, "My Daughter of the Dead Reeds"

25

2013

**SELECTED BY MIRANDA HILL;
MARK MEDLEY; RUSSELL WANGERSKY**

Steven Benstead, "Megan's Bus"

Jay Brown, "The Egyptians"

Andrew Forbes, "In the Foothills"

Philip Huynh, "Gulliver's Wife"

Amy Jones, "Team Ninja"

Marnie Lamb, "Mrs. Fujimoto's Wednesday Afternoons"

Doretta Lau, "How Does a Single Blade of Grass Thank the Sun?"

Laura Legge, "It's Raining in Paris"

Natalie Morrill, "Ossicles"

Zoey Leigh Peterson, "Sleep World"

Eliza Robertson, "My Sister Sang"

Naben Ruthnum, "Cinema Rex"*

26

2014

**SELECTED BY STEVEN W. BEATTIE;
CRAIG DAVIDSON; SALEEMA NAWAZ**

Rosaria Campbell, "Probabilities"

Nancy Jo Cullen, "Hashtag Maggie Vandermeer"

M.A. Fox, "Piano Boy"

Kevin Hardcastle, "Old Man Marchuk"

Amy Jones, "Wolves, Cigarettes, Gum"

Tyler Keevil, "Sealskin"*

Jeremy Lanaway, "Downturn"

Andrew MacDonald, "Four Minutes"

Lori McNulty, "Monsoon Season"

Shana Myara, "Remainders"

Julie Roorda, "How to Tell if Your Frog Is Dead"

Leona Theis, "High Beams"

Clea Young, "Juvenile"

27
2015
SELECTED BY ANTONY DE SA,
TANIS RIDEOUT, AND CARRIE SNYDER

Charlotte Bondy, "Renaude"

Emily Bossé, "Last Animal Standing on Gentleman's Farm"

Deirdre Dore, "The Wise Baby"*

Charlie Fiset, "Maggie's Farm"

K'ari Fisher, "Mercy Beatrice Wrestles the Noose"

Anna Ling Kaye, "Red Egg and Ginger"

Andrew MacDonald, "The Perfect Man for my Husband"

Madeleine Maillet, "Achilles' Death"

Lori McNulty, "Fingernecklace"

Sarah Meehan Sirk, "Moonman"

Ron Schafrick, "Lovely Company"

Georgia Wilder, "Cocoa Divine and the Lightning Police"

28
2016
SELECTED BY KATE CAYLEY;
BRIAN FRANCIS; MADELEINE THIEN

Carleigh Baker, "Chins and Elbows"

Paige Cooper, "The Roar"

Charlie Fiset, "If I Ever See the Sun"

Mahak Jain, "The Origin of Jaanvi"

Colette Langlois, "The Emigrants"*

Alex Leslie, "The Person You Want to See"

Andrew MacDonald, "Progress on a Genetic Level"

J.R. McConvey, "Home Range"

J.R. McConvey, "How the Grizzly Came to Hang in the Royal Oak Hotel"

Souvankham Thammavongsa, "Mani Pedi"

Souvankham Thammavongsa, "Paris"